"Will you let me enroll my son in your school?"

Mark braced himself for Alex's negative response. Only a truly desperate man would ask his ex-fiancée to provide child care for the child who—for all practical purposes—was the reason they never married. If not for Braden, Mark and Alex would probably have a kid or two of their own by now.

A little bell rang from inside the attractive ranch-style house that had almost been his. He could hear the muffled sounds of children's happy voices.

God, please let her take Bray. My son deserves a second chance...even if I don't.

Dear Reader,

People were surprised that I opened my SISTERS OF THE SILVER DOLLAR miniseries with the youngest of the Radonovic sisters' story (*Betting on Grace*, 11/05) instead of choosing the eldest. Granted, birth order might seem the most logical choice, but firstborn Alexandra wasn't as open as Grace. It took me four books to get to know Alex well, but once I did I came to love her dearly. She's weathered more loss and heartbreak than seems fair, but she hasn't let life's difficulties break her spirit.

The Quiet Child concludes my series about this Romani family, but I know these characters will always be a part of my heart, and their stories will live on in my imagination. If any of these turns into a book, I'll be sure to let you know. In the meantime, if you've missed Grace's story or Liz's (*Bringing Baby Home*, Harlequin American Romance 8/06) or Kate's (*One Daddy Too Many*, Harlequin American Romance 5/06), please visit my Web site, www.debrasalonen. com, where you can order copies of these and other backlist titles.

I draw upon a great many resources for every book I write, and since Alex owns and operates a preschool, I think it's only fair to thank all the "little" people in my life (those under the age of four)—in alphabetical order: Allexindir, Cael, Courey, Ian, Josie, Mckenzie, Madelaine, Malte, Morgan, Parker, Parker Daisy, Preston, Sayer and Spencer. And many thanks to "Miss Gail" for having the patience to introduce music—even drums—to this new crop of budding musicians.

Happy reading,

Debra

The Quiet Child
DEBRA SALONEN

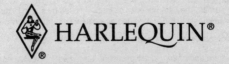

HARLEQUIN®

TORONTO • NEW YORK • LONDON
AMSTERDAM • PARIS • SYDNEY • HAMBURG
STOCKHOLM • ATHENS • TOKYO • MILAN • MADRID
PRAGUE • WARSAW • BUDAPEST • AUCKLAND

ISBN-13: 978-0-373-75143-3
ISBN-10:   0-373-75143-5

THE QUIET CHILD

www.eHarlequin.com

Printed in U.S.A.

ABOUT THE AUTHOR

As a child, Debra wanted to be an artist. She saved her allowance to send away for a "Learn To Draw" kit, but when her mother mistook Deb's artful rendition of a horse for a cow, Deb turned to her second love—writing. She credits her success as an author to her parents for giving her the chance to realize those dreams. She and her high school sweetheart, who have been married for over thirty years, live in California surrounded by a great deal of family, quite a few dogs and views that appeal to the artist still trapped in her soul.

Books by Debra Salonen

HARLEQUIN AMERICAN ROMANCE
1114—ONE DADDY TOO MANY*
1126—BRINGING BABY HOME*

HARLEQUIN SUPERROMANCE
 910—THAT COWBOY'S KIDS
 934—HIS DADDY'S EYES
 986—BACK IN KANSAS
1003—SOMETHING ABOUT EVE
1061—WONDERS NEVER CEASE
1098—MY HUSBAND, MY BABIES
1104—WITHOUT A PAST
1110—THE COMEBACK GIRL
1196—A COWBOY SUMMER
1238—CALEB'S CHRISTMAS WISH
1279—HIS REAL FATHER

SIGNATURE SELECT SAGA
BETTING ON GRACE*

*Sisters of the Silver Dollar

Don't miss any of our special offers. Write to us at the following address for information on our newest releases.

Harlequin Reader Service
U.S.: 3010 Walden Ave., P.O. Box 1325, Buffalo, NY 14269
Canadian: P.O. Box 609, Fort Erie, Ont. L2A 5X3

For the children—quiet and otherwise—
who give my life balance and perspective.
Especially my own Miss M.

Chapter One

"Itsy-bitsy spider crawled up the water spout."

Alexandra Radonovic—or Miss Alex, as the sixteen preschool-aged students grouped on the round, sunshine-yellow rug called her—hummed the second verse, letting the class fill in the words. The four-year-olds knew the song well and loudly enunciated each phrase for the benefit of their younger classmates, adding a dramatic hand gesture to the word *washed*.

"Out came the sun…hum, hum…"

"Did you forget the words, Auntie Alex?" her niece, Maya, hissed softly at Alex's elbow.

Alex smiled at the concern she heard in Maya's voice. "No, sweetheart," Alex whispered, "I was just listening to see who needed help."

Satisfied with the answer, the child smiled back.

"And the itsy-bitsy spider climbed up the spout again."

Alex led the applause. "Who's ready for outside time?"

"I am, I am." Alex's sister Liz, who'd volunteered to help that morning, jumped to her feet. Liz, who was just fourteen months younger than Alex—and extremely busy with her new herbal-tea company, *and* her recent engagement—hadn't hesitated when Alex had called in a panic. Shorthanded again.

Earlier in the year, their sister Grace had tangled with old family friend Charles Harmon, a powerful and deceitful lawyer and casino owner, who had promised revenge on the entire Radonovic clan. In Alex's case, he'd tried to stir up trouble by spreading untrue rumors about some of the people working for her at her Dancing Hippo Day Care and Preschool.

No charges were ever filed because Alex always did a thorough background check before she ever hired anyone to work at the Hippo. Although it had taken time and a great deal of talking, Alex had personally called each parent on her enrollment roster and explained what was happening. To her profound relief, the parents of her students had stood by her, one and all. Unfortunately, two of her part-time aides hadn't appreciated being the targets of slander and had quit. Alex was still trying to replace them.

She didn't blame anyone for not wanting to deal with Charles's spite, but she really couldn't afford to be short-staffed over the holidays. Stress was not only bad for the kids, it was bad for her health. And she couldn't afford to get sick. Not now.

"You're a lifesaver, Liz," Alex said, helping to escort the energetic herd of youngsters toward the back door after the mandatory pause for putting on coats and sweaters. Late November in Las Vegas might be balmy compared to other parts of the country, but lately the wind seemed to hold a bite that went straight to her core.

"Rita should be back soon. I can't imagine shopping for Christmas on the day after Thanksgiving, but she starts at five and buys all of the gifts for her grandchildren in one morning."

Rita, a retired kindergarten teacher, was Alex's most senior aide. Privately, she'd told Alex that she'd been planning on quitting before the Charles Harmon episode but had delayed the decision because she didn't want to add to Alex's problems.

The Dancing Hippo was Alex's baby. Her life, her sisters were quick to point out. Seven and a half years earlier, she'd opened the day-care center partly to stay afloat financially and partly to keep from sinking into an easily justified depression after her fiancé, Mark Gaylord, had broken off their relationship. Alex would never forget the day he'd admitted to spending the night with his partner, Tracey. Alex had barely come to grips with his betrayal when she learned that Tracey was pregnant.

"I didn't mean for this to happen, Alex," he'd said. "But it did and I have to accept responsibility for my actions."

Mark. Ever the hero. The love of her life. The man with the troubled past who worked so hard to rise above his difficult childhood. She knew what being a father meant to him. His concern for children had sealed her love for him, and she'd understood why he'd chosen his unborn child over her. What she'd never understood was why he'd risked their future together for a night in the arms of a woman like Tracey, who had a reputation for partying with all the wrong people.

Alex shook her head to push the thoughts of Mark away. She would have said she was over him completely if not for the fire the night of her sister Kate's wedding last July. Someone had set fire to Liz's date's home and greenhouse, and Liz—the sister who had voluntarily served in a war zone—had been too shaken up to drive, so their mother, Yetta, had asked Alex to play chauffeur.

To Alex's shock, Mark, who had apparently traded in his cop's badge to become an arson investigator, had been on the scene. Seeing him had resurrected all her old memories and she'd barely made it through a night since without bumping into him in her dreams.

"Two steps forward and five steps back," she muttered under her breath.

"Are you talking to yourself again?"

"Again? When have I ever talked to myself?" she asked Liz, who was smiling that smile Alex hated. A cross between know-it-all and smug. Not that Liz was condescending by nature, but at the moment she was on top of the world. She'd just become engaged to a great guy and her specialty blends of herbal teas seemed to be taking off.

"Alex, you're the eldest. Every time you were giving orders to Kate, Grace or me, you were talking to yourself."

Liz's laugh was so infectious Alex couldn't prevent her own guffaw. "Are you saying I was bossy?"

"You tried to be. But in all fairness, it's not your fault. Dad called you Alexandra the Great, remember? So you had a lot to live up to, and since we were your only subjects, you tried to rule us."

Alex stepped in front of three-year-old Madelaine Rose before the child could whack two-year-old Preston Johnson over the head with a plastic shovel. "We are gentle with our friends, Maddie. Treat people the way you'd like to be treated."

To Liz, she said, "I tried to lead by example, not oligarchy."

Liz laughed so hard tears came to her pretty brown eyes.

Alex had never seen her sister so relaxed and obviously happy. *Love will do that do you,* she thought wistfully.

She'd loved being in love and would have actively sought to find a new man in her life after Mark—except she'd been so busy trying not to lose the house they'd been in the process of buying together.

Without his additional income to secure the loan, she'd been forced to use the money in her trust fund to make the down payment. Even now she didn't have a lot of wiggle room when it came to budgeting, and her ongoing health issues hadn't helped matters. Self-employed, she didn't make money when she had to hire extra help because she was doubled over in pain once a month from an inflamed ovarian cyst.

But she had no real regrets when it came to her career. Instead of becoming a secondary school teacher as she'd intended, she taught preschool. She loved working with children in this fertile—everything was amazing and fresh—stage of life. She loved kids—even if she wasn't always wild about their parents. She'd learned how to handle almost every contingency, from babysitters who forgot to pick up their charge on time to parents who had restraining orders against their mates. The one thing she hadn't found was a mate of her own.

For years, she'd expected to look up one day and see Mr. Right walk through her door. After all, her mother, whose reputation as a gypsy mystic was well known, had foreseen a prophecy for each of her four daughters. Alex's was very clear: "A child's laughter can heal the wounded heart, if first you heal the child."

Child. Preschool teacher. Alex figured she was in the right place to meet the man of her prophecy. And she'd worked with dozens of kids over the years who qualified as wounded. She just hadn't fallen in love with any of their single fathers.

"Hey, did you know Grace is coming back next week?"

Alex glanced at Liz for a second, but out of the corner of her eye she detected trouble in the sandbox. She headed that way, motioning for Liz to follow. "Are you kidding? Does that mean she and Nick aren't coming for Christmas? Mom will be heartbroken."

"No, they're coming then, too. This is just Grace alone. Something to do with Charles's trial. He's trying to get it postponed again." She sighed. "I'm ready for some closure where that mess is concerned, aren't you?"

Alex nodded but was too busy redirecting William, before he could wrestle a big red dump truck out of the hands of his playmate, to answer.

Liz kept talking anyway. "Mom also said that Grace is going to train the new bookkeeper Kate and Jo hired at Romantique."

Jo Brighten, Kate's mother-in-law, had purchased Grace's share of the restaurant after Grace had moved to Detroit to be with her future husband, Nikolai.

"That's generous of Grace," Alex said.

"Especially since she misses her job so much. It's too bad she and Nick have to live in Detroit."

"Did I tell you I took my staff to dinner at Romantique two nights ago as a thank-you for hanging in with me through this horrible time? We had a wonderful meal. Jo made beef short ribs that melted in your mouth. And her seven-layer cake. Oh, my G—" Alex stopped mid-exclamation. "Morgan, what are you doing? MacKensie is your friend. She doesn't want sand in her hair. Do you, MacKensie?"

She took both little girls into her arms and settled the

dispute, which was more about them both being three than anything else. "Bend over, MacKensie, and shake like a wet dog. Can you do that for me? Good girl."

To Liz, she said, "Sorry. Would you do me a favor? Go inside and start setting out the snack. Carrots and raisins, I think. This week's menu is up on the wall in the kitchen."

She smiled as she watched her sister wind her way through the boisterous youngsters in the yard. Liz's sense of joy showed in the way she walked, talked and took time to comfort the little girl who tripped and fell in her path.

Just twenty minutes till nap time, Alex thought as she scanned the yard, making a mental head count of her charges. Once, early in her career, she'd "lost" a child who had crawled into a toy box and gone to sleep while the adults had called 9-1-1. Now, some sixth sense kept her connected with her charges.

"We did it," Liz said in a stage whisper half an hour later. "The entire herd, down for the count."

"Yep. Another exciting morning in the world of child-care," Alex joked as she walked her sister to the front door. "I really appreciate your lending a hand, Liz."

They stepped outside on the wide, covered stoop that faced the street. A chain-link fence, a four-foot-tall version of the one that enclosed the play yard at the rear of the house, followed the sidewalk. The hinged gate opened to a wheel-chair-friendly ramp leading to the door. Alex hired a yard service to keep her two matching rectangles of grass alive beneath the brutal Las Vegas sun each summer. In the middle of the yard to the left was a hand-carved sign carrying her logo—a dancing hippopotamus in a purple tutu.

"No problem. David, I mean, Paul—" Liz smacked the heel of her hand to her forehead in exasperation. "I can't believe I'm still having trouble remembering my husband-to-be's real name. That sounds terrible, doesn't it?"

Alex smiled. David, the name everyone in the family had first known him as, had been hiding his past to escape a vindictive maniac. Once that man was no longer a threat, David had begun resurrecting his former persona, Paul McAffey—the man Liz was planning to marry.

They hadn't set a date, but they had moved in together.

"Speaking of Paul, how goes his new position at UNLV?"

"He won't actually be teaching until next semester, thank God. But even getting things ready has been a full-time job. I think he's going to be brilliant, but I could be prejudiced. Gotta run. We have a huge tea order to fill today, and if I'm not there, Lydia and Reezira might not get the ratio of herbs right. We're still overcoming a language barrier although they're catching on pretty fast."

Liz's two employees were one-time illegal immigrants who had been secreted into the United States by Charles Harmon and forced into prostitution. Two more examples of people who had wound up suffering because of one man's greed and lust for power. But, thanks to Liz, the young women now had green cards and a job.

Alex started to ask if the girls were going to join the family for the holidays, but the sound of a car door closing caught her attention.

Liz let out an audible gasp. Alex's breath caught in her throat, making speech impossible.

Mark.

"Wow. He looks different without his firefighter gear on. Handsomer. Is that a word?"

"Dunno."

"What's he doing here?"

"I have no idea."

"Well, um, I'll stick around. Just in case."

Alex looked at her sister and smiled. She and Liz had always shared a special bond. Growing up, each had seemed to sense when the other was upset or in trouble. But that bond had weakened, for several reasons. One was the man coming up her walk. Liz had been quicker to forgive than Alex had thought appropriate.

"No. You've got more important things to do."

"But—"

"I know what you're thinking, Elizabeth," she said, using the formal tone their mother always employed. "But don't worry. I can handle him."

"But—"

"Tell Paul I said hi."

Liz left, pausing only long enough to mutter something to Mark on her way past, then she hurried across the street where her new SUV was parked.

The gate made a familiar creaking sound as Mark opened it to walk up the ramp. "Hi, Alex."

"Hello, Mark. This is a surprise."

"Yeah, I'm sure it is. I probably should have called first, but I thought I'd take a chance…um…do you have a minute? I could come back later."

She poked her head inside to make sure her helpers had everything under control—and to give her heart a chance to quit turning somersaults. Why did he have to look so damn good? Blue jeans, black mock turtleneck and black leather jacket. He'd aged some, but every line gave his face more character. He wasn't just a handsome young stud—he was a man.

She'd been doing this job for so long that she could tell

at a glance that the children were resting peacefully and her aides were preparing for the afternoon session.

She closed the door and leaned against it, crossing her arms. The late fall sunshine was warming; the wind was blocked by the house behind her. "Now is as good a time as any. What can I do for you?"

"Right to the point, as always. Okay, then, here's my question. Will you let me enroll my son in your school?"

MARK BRACED HIMSELF for a negative response. He had no right to ask the question, but he was desperate. Only a truly desperate man would ask his ex-fiancée to provide child care for the child who, for all practical purposes, was the reason they weren't married. If not for Braden, he and Alex would probably have a kid or two of their own by now.

Instead, Mark had spent nearly every minute since that fateful night when he'd given in to Tracey's no-strings-attached suggestion trying to make amends for his mistake. To his ex-wife, for not loving her enough to put up with her drinking and partying. To Braden, for not being able to pretend any longer that he loved the little boy's mother. To his conscience, which knew just how badly he'd hurt Alex.

"You want to bring your son to the Dancing Hippo?"

"Yes."

"Why? This is a preschool. Your son must be in what—second grade?"

"He's repeating first grade this year. He just turned seven. Tracey and I split up when he was three. She started him in kindergarten when he was four. His birthday is September 23, so technically he was old enough, but I didn't think he was ready."

"It didn't work out?"

"He passed, but whenever I went to a parent-teacher conference, I could tell his teacher was concerned about Bray's socialization skills—or lack of them. He's very shy and has had a bit of a stuttering problem almost since he started speaking. At the time, it wasn't debilitating, but his teacher thought he'd be better off repeating kindergarten. Tracey disagreed. She insisted that he'd catch up in first grade."

"Didn't happen?"

"Didn't have a chance to happen. About six weeks into the school year, his teacher called us both in for a conference. She was extremely blunt. She said Braden needed speech therapy and should probably be placed in a special-needs class."

Alex winced. "I bet that didn't go over well with Tracey."

"She blew up. Accused his teacher of being lazy and showing favoritism. She called me the next day and said that since she wasn't working, there was no reason why she shouldn't home-school him."

Mark looked away. In hindsight, the battle that had ensued had been a waste of time and money and had put his son right in the middle of his parents' war. "I hired a lawyer to try to make her take him to school. Odessa, Tracey's mother, got involved. I filed for sole custody. Then, in March, before we had anything settled, Tracey died."

Her mouth dropped open. "Tracey's dead?"

He nodded. "A fire. She and the man she might have been involved with at the time were killed." He didn't add the brutal details: the two had died in an explosion at a meth lab where Tracey most probably had gone to get drugs from her on-again, off-again pusher boyfriend.

"Oh, how awful. Poor Braden."

Mark hurried past her sympathy. "I put Braden back in

regular school as soon as I could. Probably the wrong thing to do. He had a hard time adjusting. The other kids teased him." *They teased him about his stutter and picked on him because he was small and weak and lost.* Mark could barely think about that time without breaking down. He'd felt like the worst father in the world.

"I know it's a cliché," Alex offered, "but kids can be cruel. Did the school test him academically?"

Mark nodded. "He's behind in reading and math skills and has problems with peer interaction—their words, not mine. His cognitive functions—" He tried to smile. "See, I've learned a new language. His cognitive functions are within normal range, but his speech impediment has had a negative impact on his ability to make friends and communicate with his teachers. We have an IEP—Individualized Education Plan—designed to help him get back on track."

The concerned look on her face intensified. "Has he shown any improvement?"

"Not really. The school he's attending likes to mainstream its special-needs students. He's in a new first-grade class and he works with a speech therapist a couple of times a week, but she's not having a lot of success. Most of the time, he just doesn't talk."

Sympathy sparkled like tears in her gorgeous brown eyes. He'd always said he could see his forever in Alex's eyes. But he'd been wrong. And now, he didn't want sympathy. He wanted—he needed—help.

"I'm looking for after-school care. Your ad in the Yellow Pages says that's something you offer. I checked with his school and the bus can drop him off here, if you'll let him come."

She frowned. "I've had a few older kids—mostly siblings of students in my preschool class—sign up for that program, but at the moment, my cousin's son is my only after-school student. Luca is pretty independent. Does his homework then plays video games until his dad picks him up. Your son would probably benefit from a more one-on-one type of program, and, frankly, I don't have the staff for that."

She hadn't said no, exactly. "He needs a place where he can feel safe and get some stimulation beyond sitting in front of the boob tube. He doesn't act out. He's not disruptive. The poor kid has missed out on a lot of things in his short life, including preschool. His mother was too busy or too broke—according to her—to enroll him in one. This kind of setting might be really good for him."

"What are you doing for child care now?"

"I have a babysitter who comes to my house. But she's found a job that pays more and given notice. I advertised the position, but I've only had a couple of applicants, and Braden didn't seem to like any of them."

Thumbing through the Yellow Pages one evening, he'd spotted Alex's ad. A quick call to his friend Zeke Martini confirmed that Alex owned and operated the Dancing Hippo.

"How many days per week would you want him to come here? What hours? If I remember correctly, a cop's shifts are pretty irregular."

Questions were good. Better than a flat-out *no*. Better than he deserved. "I'm an arson investigator with the Las Vegas Fire Department. I work five eight-and-a-half-hour days with the third Monday off. Sometimes, I might get called in if there's an emergency. There's a woman in my building who is a stay-at-home mom. She helps out if that happens, but she doesn't want to take on another kid full-time."

"So, you're just interested in after-school care, five days a week?"

"From three to six or six-thirty, depending on traffic."

Her frown made him wonder what she was thinking. Was she remembering that day when their plans had blown up into tiny shards of anger and disappointment? The day he'd told her that Tracey was pregnant, and he was the father?

"On rare occasions I might run late. I have to know there's a safety net in place in case something comes up at work. If I don't work, I can't afford to pay for after-school care. It's a vicious circle."

Her chocolate-brown eyes looked troubled. He knew how much she adored kids. But could she look past what had been between the two of them?

"Won't he feel humiliated by associating with babies? And I'm not trained to work with speech impediments."

"I wouldn't expect you to. He probably won't say two words to you while he's here. And, honestly, I think being around younger kids would be a relief for him."

A little bell rang from inside the attractive ranch-style house that had—almost—been his. He could hear the muffled sounds of children's voices. Happy sounds. *God, he prayed, please let her take Bray. He deserves a second chance. I know I don't, but Braden does.*

"I really can't say for sure, Mark. Not until I've met him. Could you bring him by sometime next week? He might not like it here at all."

"He will."

Mark believed that—although he couldn't say for sure why. He'd tried everything to communicate with his son and still didn't have a clue what was going on inside that adorable blond head. Bray looked so much like his mother it was unnerving at times. Alex might not be able to get past that—she was human, after all. But maybe she'd take pity on the poor kid, and let the past stay where it was—buried beneath angry charges and a surfeit of tears.

"How 'bout Monday? That's my day off."

Her eyes widened as if regretting her offer. "I…I don't know if this is a good idea—given our history, but okay. Bring him in. If he's not unhappy here, then we'll see."

We'll see. A small glimmer of hope, but more than he'd had in weeks. He'd take it.

"BRADEN, EAT YOUR HOT DOG. There's ketchup. You love ketchup, remember?"

Mark wasn't certain that statement was true. He'd seen Braden eat hot dogs with ketchup and assumed the boy still liked the food, but he had a feeling he could have put ketchup-covered beetles on the plate and Braden would eat them just as readily.

Braden generally did what he was told. He didn't talk back. He objected to taking a bath most nights, but Mark didn't think that made him unique. He ate, slept—except for the nightmares that hit like clockwork—and watched TV like a normal kid. But Mark knew in his gut his child wasn't "normal."

Something had happened in Braden's short life that had left him traumatized. Considering Tracey's erratic behavior during their marriage—and her turbulent, high-drama relationship with her mother—the possibilities were endless. Mark had been a cop for four years before he'd switched to arson. He'd seen enough cases of child abuse to fear the worst.

Hell, Mark had lived through the worst himself. The son

of an alcoholic father and codependent mother, Mark had found himself on the receiving end of many a beating. "You're a total screwup," his father would shout. But Mark had joined the police academy, found a mentor who believed in him, and had eventually moved to Las Vegas and met Alex.

Then, he'd blown it. How his old man would have laughed if he hadn't managed to fall asleep with a burning cigarette and set fire to the house, killing himself and Mark's mother.

After Mark and Alex had broken up, he'd married Tracey in a quick civil ceremony. A few months later, he'd taken the necessary tests to become a fireman. He'd changed jobs so Tracey's position in the department wouldn't be in conflict after she came back from maternity leave—and maybe to some degree because of what had happened to his parents. Serendipitously, he'd discovered his true calling—arson investigation.

Unfortunately, Tracey's life hadn't gone so well. Trouble at work, trouble keeping a qualified babysitter, trouble with her mother, trouble with her marriage. Tracey had sunk into a depression, and nothing Mark said or did seemed to help.

Mark loved his son, but any tender feelings he'd tried to coax to life for Tracey had died before their son was a year old. At some level, Mark had known that she'd sensed his ambivalence about their marriage, and she'd blamed Alex for it. Her anger slowly poisoned her whole life. An altercation with a junkie during an arrest brought her under scrutiny for excess use of force. She probably would have been kicked off the force in disgrace if she hadn't been injured in the scuffle. Chronic pain may have added to her need for alcohol and street drugs.

Mark was still picking up the pieces of the wreck he'd made of his life. The only good thing to come of his mistake was Braden, but at the moment, he felt very close to losing his son. His gut told him Alex Radonovic—dauntless advocate of children, and the kindest, most loving person he'd ever known—was his last hope.

Chapter Two

"Please tell me you're joking," Kate said at the weekly gathering of sisters. Kate and Liz—Grace sometimes joined them by phone from Detroit, but hadn't called that morning—were already seated at their mother's kitchen table when Alex arrived.

She'd gotten off to a bad start when her newest hire had called in sick. Fortunately, a substitute aide had been available to fill in.

This would cost Alex extra, but she'd pay it gladly. Today was the day Mark was bringing his son to her school. A fact that she'd just shared with her sisters.

"Are we talking the same Mark who broke your heart?"

Alex made a face. "That's ancient history. And it's not as if I'm enrolling Mark. After-school care only. I think I can handle that…if his little boy likes it here."

"What's not to like?" Liz asked. "Every kid I know loves the Hippo."

Alex smiled her thanks. "Mark's son has some special needs. His name is Braden, by the way. He sounds… wounded. Poor little guy. His mother is dead, you know."

"Dead?" Liz croaked, nearly choking on a sip of tea. "I hadn't heard that. How?"

Alex shrugged. "I didn't ask for details. Mark seemed so…I don't know, defeated. Really not the way I remember him."

The old Mark, the man she'd fallen in love with the first time they'd met at a New Year's Eve party at Sam's Town casino when he and a couple of buddies had crashed her family's party, had been brash and edgy and so handsome he could have been a model. Her first thought had been *He could be Romani.* But he wasn't. Worse, he was a cop. A fact that had become an issue between Alex and her father.

Changing the subject, she looked at Kate. "Mom said Romantique is booked solid through the holidays. That's great. Are we still doing the charity dinner on Christmas Day?"

Kate nodded, her curly hair fluttering in an unstyled mess that made her look waiflike. "Unless I collapse first. Was I this tired when I was living at home?"

Liz grinned. "You didn't have a husband when you lived here, but it's not too late to come back. Reezira and Lydia aren't moving in until next weekend."

Since Liz had a new roommate—Paul, her fiancé—the two young Romanian women had decided it was time to strike out on their own. When Yetta had offered to let them rent Kate's and Maya's former rooms, they'd jumped at the chance.

Kate looked toward the hallway as if missing her old sanctuary. "Are they excited?"

"Delirious," Liz said. "They're convinced Vegas is way hipper than Henderson. Plus, Alex has promised them extra work at the Hippo any time the tea business is slow."

"Don't they need credentials to work in child-care?"

"I can always use a hand making snacks, handling the sign-in desk and prepping for art projects. I keep dreaming of finding someone like Jo, who will step in and handle things when I need a day off."

Kate's mother-in-law had gone through a difficult period health-wise that had included a misdiagnosis of lung cancer, but she was on the mend now and fully committed to the restaurant.

Kate nodded in agreement. "Jo is a gift. That's for sure. And once we get the paperwork side of things covered, I'll be able to breathe again."

Alex was about to ask about their new bookkeeper—she was thinking about hiring some part-time clerical help herself—when Kate sighed and said, "That is if I can get Maya back on track. Why didn't anyone warn me about the terrible fives?"

Maya was turning five in February.

"She can't help it that she's an adult in a child's body," Alex said with a chuckle. "Have you broken the news that she's going to a new school after the first of the year?"

Kate stood up and started to pace. "We drove by it on Friday after I picked her up at the Hippo. She called it an Ugly Duckling school and flat-out refuses to go."

"Change is tough at that age," Alex said. Or any age. She wondered what kind of changes a seven-year-old boy would bring to her school's dynamic.

Mark had called the night before and left a message on her answering machine, confirming that he'd be bringing his son in today. His voice had the power to transport her back to an earlier time in her life. A glorious, hopeful time when she'd been blissfully in love. Until the day Mark had shown up and couldn't look her in the eye. Her gypsy ESP had known immediately that something bad had happened. Even before he could confess, she'd seen the shadow of another woman draped around him. Blond. Curvaceous. Sexy.

"You were with Tracey," Alex had charged.

He hadn't bothered to deny it. But he'd pleaded with her to give him another chance. At the time, Alex had been too hurt to consider reconciliation, and when she'd finally called him to talk, he'd told her there was a baby on the way.

Mark had married Tracey.

"I'd take back that night with my soul, if I could," Mark had told her—just days before his scheduled nuptials.

"If you had one," Alex had cried, wishing she could hurt him as much as he'd hurt her.

"Alexandra."

Alex looked up at her mother's voice. Yetta had apparently entered the kitchen through the door that opened into the garage. She was in the process of hanging up her coat, and from the concerned look on her face must have said Alex's name more than once.

"Oh, hi, Mom. I thought you were at the cemetery."

"That was yesterday. Are you feeling okay?"

Alex felt her cheeks heat up. The last thing she wanted was for someone to bring up her health issues. "Yes, I'm fine. Just a lot on my mind. You know how the holidays are."

"Which parents are volunteering today?" Liz asked. "Not Mrs. Moorehouse, I hope."

A slight twinge in her stomach made Alex shift in her seat. Parents who volunteered to help a certain number of hours each month received a reduced rate for their child's fee. Roberta Moorehouse was a beautiful woman who seemed to be vying for the title of CEO of motherhood. Her intensity wore Alex down faster than twenty kids on a sugar high.

"The Moorehouse family went back east for Thanksgiving. Roberta offered to come in twice next week to make up."

Her sisters looked at each other and snickered.

"Will Mark volunteer?" Liz asked.

Alex hadn't considered that possibility. "I don't know. He hasn't even enrolled his son, yet. Besides, the fee schedule is different for after-school students. Are we having breakfast?"

After sharing a skillet of scrambled eggs, the three sisters went their separate ways, with Yetta accompanying Alex down the street to her house. They cut through the back gate to her private entrance. French doors led to her suite, which included a sitting room, kitchenette and large bath. The rest of the house—except for the small guest room that doubled as an office—was devoted to the Dancing Hippo, but this was Alex's personal domain.

"Alexandra, I'm worried about you," her mother said before Alex could open the door. "You've been in my dreams lately. Something is shifting in your life, but I can't tell if the change is for the good. How is your health?"

Alex rested her shoulder against the stucco. Car engines and children's laughter coming from the street told her it was almost time to become Miss Alex. Miss Alex didn't have time for Gypsy mysticism—that was Grace's thing.

"Mom, the holidays are coming. Christmas, Hanukkah, Kwanzaa, the solstice—one major art project after another. Before you know it, we'll be celebrating Cinco de Mayo again. I don't have time to be sick, so I won't. Period."

Her mother smiled, but there was worry in her eyes, too. "Does that mean you're still going through with your plan?"

Like any good mother, Yetta fretted when her child was in pain. Alex's experience with recurrent ovarian cysts six years earlier had given them both a lot to worry about. Because the monthly agony had sent her to bed with strong drugs and a heating pad, Alex had gone along with her doctor's suggestion that she have laparoscopic surgery to remove the seven-centimeter paratubal cyst that had been plaguing her.

Unfortunately, the benign procedure had wound up costing Alex a small fortune when she'd developed a post-surgical infection. She'd been forced to return to the hospital for ten days of around-the-clock IV antibiotics, followed by several more weeks of out-patient treatment to pack and drain the inflamed incision. There had been talk of cosmetic surgery to fix the scar on her belly, but Alex had had enough of doctors and hospitals.

Since that time, she'd been taking high-dosage birth-control pills to prevent ovulation. Current medical belief held that you could prevent the formation of cysts by keeping the ovaries from functioning. Only Yetta knew that Alex recently had stopped taking the pill.

"Mom, we've been through this. I've weighed the benefits against the risks. I hate dumping all those hormones into my body every month. With luck, we'll discover that my body is over that phase where it needed to grow annoying little cysts every month."

"I'm meddling, dear, aren't I?" her mother asked. "I'm sorry. It's the mother in me."

A twisting sensation in her pelvis—very close to her ovaries—made Alex wince. She hadn't told anyone—even her mother—the *other* reason she'd stopped taking birth-control pills.

Yetta opened the door and walked inside. "Did you have a particular story you wanted me to tell this morning?"

Her mother occasionally filled in for Alex during the opening group session so Alex could catch up on paperwork. The children loved Yetta's stories and songs. So had Alex as a child. Yetta was a wonderful mother. Alex hoped she'd be equally as good—sooner rather than later.

The day disappeared in a blur. The usual runny noses and students who needed snuggling. One or two issues with glue during the construction paper–wreath art project. One bounced check and a tearfully contrite mom whose ex was late with child support. Not an uncommon story.

Alex hadn't given up on the idea of marriage and a two-parent family. Her sisters seemed to have found their ideal mates, but some days, after listening to three or four successive matrimonial horror stories, she couldn't help but fear that her elusive Mr. Right was lost on some mysterious island.

And she was tired of waiting. She'd stopped taking her prescribed birth-control pills not because of a fear of cancer, but because she wanted to have a baby.

Liz and Paul were talking about adopting a child from India. It wouldn't be long before Grace started nesting, and Kate's new husband had openly expressed a desire to give Maya a baby brother or sister.

With no potential mate on the horizon, Alex had decided she had to take matters into her own hands. Her doctor felt there was no reason why Alex's one healthy ovary couldn't provide a viable egg, which could be artificially inseminated.

Now, it was just a matter of picking the right donor, she thought, studying the list of bios on her computer screen.

She'd print a list of her top ten choices and try to make her final selection tonight.

"Knock, knock," a deep voice called from the doorway.

Alex glanced up from her computer. The cheerful rainbow that framed the opening was a visual oxymoron to the pitch-black sky of late November that provided the backdrop for the man standing there. He was dressed all in black, too.

"Come in," she said, quickly exiting the Web site.

She stood up and walked around her desk so she could see the youngster at his side.

Practically swallowed up by a red down jacket, knitted cap and gloves, the boy seemed smaller than a seven-year-old. Like a toddler mannequin wearing big-kid clothes, she thought.

His chin remained squished to his chest as she approached. "Welcome to the Dancing Hippo, Braden," she said. "It's nice and cozy in here. You can hang your coat on any of those pegs over there." She pointed toward the small anteroom her students called Cubbyland.

She waited to see if he would do as she requested or not. He didn't budge until his father took his shoulders between his large hands and gently, but firmly, maneuvered Braden toward the cheerfully painted nook where each child had a wooden cubicle and hook. Above each box was a frame that held a sample of the student's art.

Braden stumbled slightly as he looked around. He removed his mittens and dropped them on the floor. His coat pooled at his feet, and he made no attempt to hang it up. He didn't seem to notice that he still had his cap pulled low around his forehead, completely covering his hair and eyebrows.

The red hat made his eyes stand out. Big and blue like

his mother's. The thick black lashes were Mark's contribution, Alex guessed. At first glance, Braden didn't look much like Mark, but she thought she detected certain similarities in his frame and the cast of his jaw.

"I'm so glad to meet you, Braden. My name is Miss Alex. Would you like to sit down or look around?"

Two choices. Nice and simple.

He looked at his father for guidance.

"Let's sit a minute, bud. I don't know about you, but I'm pooped."

She pointed to the center of the sunshine-yellow rug that served as the meeting circle for group activities. Alex took her usual place atop a purple hippopotamus-shaped pillow. Mark sat a few feet away at the three-o'clock position. Braden either didn't see or didn't care about the line. He sat down slightly in front of his father.

Alex folded her hands in her lap. "So, Braden, how old are you?"

He didn't acknowledge the question.

"You know how old you are, Bray. Tell her."

Braden kept his focus on his shoes, but Alex had a feeling he was also looking at her. She found this encouraging and smiled at Mark. "Maybe Braden would like to do one of my puzzles." She stood up. "I have a really cool one at the table over by my desk. Will you come with me, Braden?"

She squatted beside him and offered her hand. The little boy took it without looking up. She led him to the table and set him up with a large, bright barnyard-animal puzzle. The corresponding animal made a sound when the correct piece was placed in position.

An overly simple puzzle for a seven-year-old, but Braden didn't make any attempt to solve it. In fact, he jumped slightly when Alex put in a piece and the donkey brayed.

Yep, his hearing works fine, she thought.

"Is he taking any medication?" she asked Mark, who had followed them to the table but hadn't sat down.

"Not at the moment."

Alex leaned over and picked up the piece shaped like a cow. "What animal is this, Braden? Is it a horse?"

His lips twitched slightly. Maya would have rolled her eyes and said, "You're silly, Auntie Alex. That's a cow."

Braden didn't speak, but he did look at Alex for the first time. "What sound does a cow make, Braden? Does it moo? I bet you knew that."

His blue eyes fairly twinkled until his father sat down across from them. Even though Mark looked sort of silly with his knees pushed almost to his chest, Braden didn't smile.

"His speech therapist gives him flash cards to practice at night, but we aren't having much luck with them, are we, Bray?"

"Ask his teacher to make sure they're in his backpack when he leaves school. If I have time, I'd be happy to try them."

Mark had been hoping she'd say that. He was certain he didn't have the patience or skills to help his son. Hell, his bumbling attempts to coax his son into speaking might even have made the boy's stutter worse.

"This is a nice place, Alex. Looks a lot different than I remember from when…" He stopped. She probably didn't need to be reminded that they'd first made an offer on this house as a couple. An engaged couple.

She was patiently waiting for Braden to show some interest in the puzzle. The silence between them made him say, "We should probably get all the old sh—stuff between us cleared up, shouldn't we?"

She glanced up at him. "No. I don't think so. You're here for your son, and I'd never let my personal feelings get in the way of how I care for a child."

He knew that. But he needed to make her understand how sorry he was for what had happened between them. "I just figured if we set the record straight we wouldn't keep bumping into the elephant."

The elephant. Alex was shocked that he remembered.

When they'd first got engaged, Alex had been attending a church that required couples to participate in weekly counseling groups before they could set the date for their vows. The facilitator, a reformed alcoholic, had structured the meeting after the twelve-step model and had often likened unaddressed problems to an elephant in the living room—a giant beast that took up a great deal of space and could easily squash the best of intentions.

She cleared her throat and sat up a little straighter. "There are no elephants here, Mark. Are there, Braden?" she asked the little boy who was staring at her.

Their gazes met. And Alex felt a connection. Just for a second, but in that tiny space of time, she felt the little boy's turmoil and fear. He was terrified by demons, real and imagined.

He might not speak, but his eyes said something Alex couldn't ignore. "Help me."

"He can start here tomorrow, if you want," she heard herself tell Braden's father.

A silent thump echoed between them.

Yeah, so she'd lied about the elephant. There was a big one sitting right there on the middle of the sunshine rug, but what kind of mother would turn her back on a child in need?

She would do her best for Braden. Braden's dad, though, was on his own.

Chapter Three

"What did you say?" Mark asked, afraid he might not have heard her right.

She gently touched Braden's cheek and when he lifted his chin, she said to him, "Braden, I'd like very much for you to come to school here. There will be children who are younger than you. Some are much younger, but they will be doing different activities most of the time. You will be in my after-school program."

Mark's heart lightened with relief. "That's great news, isn't it, Braden?" He didn't wait for an answer that he knew wouldn't be forthcoming.

He helped his son get to his feet. "No more babysitters for you, Bray. You're too big for that. Now, you'll ride the bus here after school. I'll go to your school and make sure it's all set up tomorrow."

Braden seemed to be listening, but he didn't give any outward sign that he cared one way or the other. Mark was used to that lack of response. He continued to talk as if his son had answered positively, "Cool, Dad. I can't wait."

He led Braden into the coatroom. "I have a good feeling about this, Bray. I think you're going to like it here."

Alex, Mark noted, was standing to one side, a concerned look on her face. Sympathy, he figured. Maybe a tiny bit of regret or fear about what she'd opened herself up to, but when they returned to the main room, she handed him a folder, already labeled Braden Gaylord.

"Paperwork. Fee chart. Emergency contact numbers. Medical information that I might need in case something happens. Standard stuff."

When he took it from her, their fingers touched. Briefly. Maybe more of a ghost touch, but one he felt all the way through his bones. God, he'd missed her.

"Ready, buddy?" Mark asked as Alex dropped to one knee to help Braden put on his stocking cap. She tucked his hair, which Mark could have sworn they'd just got cut, out of his eyes. There was something inherently motherly in the gesture.

"Tomorrow, then," he said when she returned to her feet. "You're sure?"

Her lips pressed together in a way he knew meant she was irked. "I wouldn't have offered if I didn't think Braden and I were going to get along just fine."

"Do you think…?" He stopped. Partly because he knew it was too soon to hope; partly because he didn't want to hear that she was just being sympathetic to a motherless little boy. Alex was kind. And generous. And Mark had no business wishing the things he did.

"Okay, then, we'll see you tomorrow. Tell Miss Alex goodbye, Braden."

His son wiped his mitten across his nose and looked at the floor.

Alex smiled and patted Braden's shoulder in a supportive way. "Have a good night. I'll be on the corner waiting for you when you get off the bus. I promise." She made a cross-your-heart motion that made Braden look up. "Don't forget your flash cards tomorrow. We'll play a game with them."

Mark could tell that Alex was tired and anxious for them to leave, but he wasn't looking forward to the night ahead. A silent dinner. An evening of one-sided conversation with a little boy he loved more than life. A little boy he couldn't reach.

But he was an adult. This was his problem, not Alex's. "I'll fill out these papers and put the file in his backpack," he told her. "But I'll pay you when I come to pick him up, okay?"

"Of course."

Of course. There really wasn't anything else to say.

She opened the door. "Have a good night."

Her tone was distant. Professional.

"You, too. Thanks."

He and Braden walked down the ramp and passed through the squeaky gate. The brisk night air helped him retrieve some control over his emotions.

This was a job to her. Braden was her student. And Mark was a bad memory. That she could put their history behind her and act in Braden's best interest further proved what Mark had always known—Alex was a much better person than he was.

Besides, he told himself as he buckled his son into his seat belt, *Braden is my chief priority at the moment. My only priority.*

As he pulled away from the curb, his cell phone rang. Traffic was light, but he didn't like talking on the phone while driving, so he pulled over and put his Ford Focus into Park. "This will just take a minute, son. Then we'll stop at McDonald's for dinner, okay?"

Braden was staring out the window, his chin turned so

he could see the Christmas lights that adorned the Dancing Hippo sign. Maybe Bray would enjoy driving around at night during the holiday season to see the Christmas displays, Mark thought, making a mental reminder.

He opened his phone. "Gaylord."

"We have a situation."

Mark recognized the voice. His old friend and mentor, Zeke Martini. Zeke had been instrumental in Mark's move to Vegas nearly ten years ago. He'd helped Mark find his place in Metro and even supported Mark's move to the fire department. Mark was pretty sure it was Zeke's recommendation that had got Mark into the arson division. "What kind of situation?"

"Ritter in Vice just called. Said two of his deep cover officers busted a mid-level porn distributor and came across a good-sized stash of drugs. Locally manufactured meth. Some cocaine and some bootlegged prescription drugs. The guy is looking at his third strike and would sell out his mother if it got him some concessions."

"So?"

"He said he could prove that a former cop killed his wife by blowing up her dealer's lab…with her in it."

A cold chill passed down Mark's spine. He glanced in the backseat at his son. Braden's eyes were closed and he seemed to have nodded off, with his head resting against the cold glass.

"And…"

"He named names. Tracey. And you."

Mark squeezed his eyes shut and swallowed the swearword that automatically came to his lips. Screwed again. Even from the grave his ex-wife seemed bound and determined to make him pay for the crime of not loving her.

ALEX PUT AWAY THE PUZZLE and pushed in the chairs Mark
and Braden had been using. Before turning off the lights
in the preschool—the area of the house that would have
served as the dining and living rooms if this were a con-
ventional home, she paused to take a deep breath.

Mark. She could still smell him. Nothing as obtuse as
cologne, although he'd been known to splash on a little
Calvin Klein when they'd been dating, but a scent uniquely
him. She once jokingly called it his policeman smell. He'd
been offended until she'd assured him the pheromones
turned her on.

Oddly buoyed by the memory, she walked to her suite
and heated up a bowl of microwaveable soup. She could
have gone across the street and eaten with her mother, but
she didn't want to face her mother's questions. In her present state of mind, Alex might reveal her decision to have
a baby. And she wasn't ready to do that.

For years, she'd convinced herself that working with
kids was all she needed to feel good about her life, but now
she wanted more. And if her plan had flaws, she didn't
want to have them pointed out.

She was about to turn on the television—*Could my life
be any more boring?*—when the doorbell rang. She left her
soup on the counter and dashed to the front of the house,
her heart racing. *Mark?*

Through the peephole she could see three people—one
large and two small. The adult in the group was her cousin,
Gregor, who lived across the street.

"Alex, hi. Sorry to bother you, but your mom isn't home
and I need a favor."

"What's up?" Alex asked, opening the door wide
enough for them to enter. Nine-year-old Luca was nearly

a foot taller than his five-year-old sister, Gemilla. Both had slightly petulant looks on their faces.

"I just got a call from Montevista. MaryAnn is having a bad night. Her doctor isn't answering his page and the nurses thought I could help calm her down."

Greg's wife, MaryAnn, had suffered a complete break- down last May and had been committed by a judge for ob- servation and treatment. Although she'd been accused of committing blackmail and was partially responsible for Grace getting shot, MaryAnn was not a bad person.

"That's too bad. I thought she looked really good at Thanksgiving." Greg had brought his wife home on a three-hour pass to dine with the family. She'd seemed... distant, but calm.

"I know. But she kinda went into a slump after that. Her doctor said that kind of yo-yo thing wasn't uncommon with people suffering from clinical depression. The aide who called said she won't quit crying. I...I really need to run out there. Would you mind watching the kids?"

She opened her arms and Gemilla ran to her. "This is great. I was just fixing a really bad bowl of soup. Have you guys eaten? How 'bout pizza and a video at your house?"

Greg blinked rapidly. "You're a saint, cousin. Thanks. I'll call you as soon as I know something."

Two hours later, Alex was snuggled under a thick throw on Gregor's couch, squeezed between a little girl who was sound asleep and a little boy who was intently focused on a movie from the family's collection. *Ghostbusters.* Good for a laugh, she'd figured.

Instead of watching the antics onscreen, she studied Luca's profile. "There's going to be a new boy coming to my after-school program tomorrow," she told him quietly.

He glanced at her, his dark eyes narrowing. "Who?"

"His name is Braden. He's younger than you. His father is an arson investigator."

"A cop?" His tone held utter disdain.

"I believe he's with the fire department, but you can ask him if you're curious."

"I hate cops. They arrested my mom."

"The police who were at the marina that day saved your mother's life. And Grace's. And they helped rescue Maya when her father took her away." She paused. "Luca, what's going on? Have you been talking to your grandpa?"

His gaze dropped and his cheeks flushed.

Oh, Uncle Claude, when will you let go of the old antipathy between Gypsies and the police? Her father, Ernst, and his younger brother, Claude, had been vocal opponents of all things having to do with law enforcement for as long as Alex could remember. Her mother had once explained that Ernst had been arrested as a young man—a clear case of racial profiling before the term had become commonplace. When Alex had first started dating Mark, she'd been afraid her father might have the young cop roughed up to discourage him from seeing her. Though that hadn't happened, Ernst had never warmed to her choice of fiancé. Although, to his credit, her father never said, "I told you so," after she and Mark had broken up.

"Listen, sweetie, I know how much you miss your mom. I miss her, too. But hopefully she'll be better soon and will be able to come home for good. Braden isn't that lucky. His mother died in an accident. His dad is like your dad—trying his best to be both a mother and a father, but Mark and Braden don't have a Romani family like ours around to help out. Maybe that's why Braden has a problem."

"Huh?"

"You've been around the Hippo long enough to know that some children stutter a bit when they're first learning to speak. Well, Braden never outgrew that. In fact, his stuttering has gotten worse, and his father told me some of the kids at his school have made fun of him. So, now, he doesn't even try to talk."

Luca returned his gaze to the movie. After a minute, he sank down a bit more on the couch. He mumbled something. Fortunately, Alex had become quite adept at hearing children's whispers.

"I'll play with him," he'd said.

She smiled and gently smoothed down a cowlick in his thick black hair. Maybe with Luca's help, they'd be able to reach this quiet child and bring a little light to the boy's sad, haunted eyes. Alex knew that sometimes friendship and family could be the best medicine of all.

Chapter Four

Alex pushed back the cuff of her heavy cotton sweater to check the time. The bus from Braden's school should have been here by now.

She'd called the school herself that morning to make sure they knew to bring the little boy to the Hippo and had been reassured that Mr. Gaylord had everything set up.

Of course, he would have, she'd thought. Mark was one of the most organized, responsible men she'd ever met. Which was one reason his tryst with Tracey had hurt and baffled Alex so much. He wasn't an impulsive person, but one impulsive act had changed both of their lives forever.

A low rumble from a block away made her step to the curb and look toward the sound. "The wheels on the bus go round and round, round and round," she sang before she could stop herself.

Darn, now that tune will be in my head for hours. One of the hazards of working with preschoolers every day, she knew.

But the thought disappeared the instant the door of the bus opened. A few seconds later a boy in a familiar jacket appeared at the top of the steps. He hesitated and looked over his shoulder at the bus driver, who nodded and said, "This is your stop, Braden. See you tomorrow."

Alex had never met this particular bus driver before, but she believed in building a good rapport with everyone who had anything to do with the children she cared for, so she hopped up to the bottom step and held out her hand. "I'm Alex. I run the Hippo."

The driver was female, about Alex's age and African-American. She leaned over and shook hands. "Nice to meet you. Take good care of this little guy. He doesn't say much, but he's a sweetheart."

"Will do," Alex said, smiling down at her new charge. From her pocket, she produced a napkin that was carefully folded around one of the peanut-butter cookies that her pre-school class had made that morning. "Here. I almost forgot."

The woman's eyes lit up. "Thanks. I love cookies."

"Me, too," Alex said. To Braden, she asked, "What about you, young Mr. Gaylord? Are you ready for a snack? Milk and cookies at my place?"

He didn't answer, but she was pretty sure she saw his head bob affirmatively. She reversed direction and stepped down, making sure her foot landed on the sidewalk, not in the gutter, then she waited for Braden to follow. She would have liked to see a bit more enthusiasm in his step, but she understood how scary this move was for him.

Once they were both safely away from the bus, the driver tooted the horn then stepped on the gas. Once again the "Wheels" song popped into her mind, but she stifled it and said, "So, Braden, I see you have your backpack. That's good. Are your practice cards inside it?"

He didn't answer, but he fell into step beside her as she headed toward the Dancing Hippo's front entrance. "When we get inside," she told him, "you'll hang up your coat on a hook that has your name above it. There's a cubbyhole, too, where you can keep your things and no one else is allowed to mess with your stuff. Okay?"

He looked up. The bright afternoon sun gave her her first truly clear look at his face. He looked so much like his mother Alex fought to stifle a gasp. Alex had only met Mark's partner half a dozen times when Alex and Mark had been engaged, but the woman had left a vivid impression. Same perfect features, same beautiful blue eyes. Thankfully none of Tracey's trademark intensity was there. The woman had given off a *vibe,* for lack of a better word, that had made Alex very uncomfortable—even before she'd stolen Mark.

Ten minutes later, Alex was showing Braden to the "big kids' table," as the younger students called it, when her niece suddenly rushed up. "You brought him, Auntie Alex. Good job."

Maya often repeated words or phrases that the adults around her used. This time, the praise made Alex smile.

"Why, thank you, Maya. I told you we were having a new student join us today."

Braden had frozen at the sound of Maya's voice and was watching the little girl as if she might be a threat. Alex put a hand on his shoulder and said, "Braden, this is my niece, Maya."

"Hi," Maya said. She blushed and looked down at her patent-leather Mary Janes. Alex could honestly say she'd never seen her niece at a loss for words.

"Braden is ready for a snack, dear heart. Would you go to the small refrigerator and bring him a milk?"

"Sure."

When Maya dashed off to the other side of the room, Braden followed her with his gaze. There was a certain longing in his look that almost broke Alex's heart. Did he yearn for friendship or just release from the burdens that seemed to weigh down his thin little shoulders?

"Why don't you sit here, Braden?" she suggested, pulling out a small, plastic chair.

Braden sat down.

Alex put the flash cards that she'd found in his backpack near the middle of the table; then she walked to the kitchen area for a cookie and a napkin. When she returned, Maya was sitting beside him, chattering away.

"Auntie Alex, that's Miss Alex to you, used to be sorta… um…not fat, exactly, but not as skinny as she is today. She also danced a lot because she's a Gypsy, like me. And when she was young she heard some boy cousins giggling and laughing about her size. They called her a dancing hippo. She thought that was sooo funny that she promised herself if she ever had a business, she'd use that name. Cool, huh?"

Alex hadn't realized Maya knew the story behind the preschool's name. Not that she cared. She had been quite a bit more…voluptuous back in her teens and early twenties than she was now. Her hospitalization had melted off the pounds, not that she'd ever recommend near death as a weight-reduction program.

She'd also cut her waist-length hair at about the same time. Teaching preschool was all about simplicity, she'd learned.

She was a little surprised Mark hadn't commented on the changes he must have noticed about her. But then, she told herself, his main concern was his son.

And rightly so, she decided half an hour later after a futile attempt to get Braden to work with her using the flash cards. *If the speech therapist isn't having any luck, what made me think I could break through the little boy's wall of resistance?* she asked herself.

Deciding they both needed a diversion, she said, "Braden, I think we need some fresh air."

Maya and the twenty-five children from both the day care and preschool usually spent the last half hour of the day outside, weather permitting. Today, the sky was a watery blue with high, thin wisps of clouds. Luckily, the breeze was mild.

Over the years, she'd slowly added a variety of swings, slides, sandboxes and climbing platforms to her play yard. The children learned the rules very quickly or they weren't allowed on the equipment. She was pleased to see how cooperative they were being today.

Maya and her group of friends, which included Gregor's daughter, Gemilla, were patiently waiting a turn on the suspension bridge. Three boys—all four-year-olds—were playing pirate, battling over who was boss.

Alex let the play continue for another minute, but she could sense the little girls' growing frustration as the boys ignored their request to share the large wooden structure. She felt her new miniature shadow follow behind as she approached.

"Okay, boys, time to let the girls have a turn."

Two of the children jumped down into the sandy area below, but the third—William Moorehouse—balked. "I'm king of the pirates. You can't tell me what to do."

"Sorry, William, but I'm commander of the play yard and I have domain over all that you see. Hop down."

He crossed his arms. "No."

Inwardly, Alex groaned. Seldom had a day passed without some sort of challenge from William...or his mother.

"William," another voice said sharply.

The child lost his bluster as his mother approached. "Get down as your teacher asked. We talked about following orders, remember?" To Alex, Roberta Moorehouse said, "He's at that challenge-authority stage of life."

Her son still hadn't moved, so Alex walked up to him and looked him directly in the eye. "William, it's time to get down, so the girls have a chance to play on the bridge. Can you get down by yourself, or do you need my help?"

He looked at Roberta, first, then mumbled something Alex couldn't quite catch and scrambled down the rope steps, knocking into Maya and her friends as he passed by. Before Alex could follow and talk to him about good manners, Roberta exclaimed, "We have a new student. Hello, there. Aren't you a doll? How old are you, sweetie? Five?"

Braden drew back, his eyes wide with apprehension. Alex had no choice but to rescue him rather than follow through with William. She stepped between Braden and Roberta and said, "I plan to introduce Braden slowly so we don't overwhelm him. He's going to be joining my after-school program. He's in first grade."

Roberta had the good graces to look embarrassed by her gaffe. Before she could apologize—and probably humiliate Braden even more—Maya flew to the rescue.

The little girl launched herself from the top of the jungle gym. Fortunately, Alex was close enough to catch her, so the child made a soft landing, then Maya stepped beside Braden and put her arm around his shoulders. "He's my friend. You better be nice to him."

Roberta was obviously at a loss for words.

Braden appeared shocked, too, but he didn't push Maya away. In fact, his expression turned soft. Alex wondered if maybe he was a little in love.

Before she could say anything, Alex heard a shout and saw William standing over another student who was on his back on the grass. Roberta let out a loud, "William," saving Alex the trouble. To Maya, Alex said, "You're Braden's official buddy, okay? Show him around while I take care of this."

Two hours later, the last of her regular students had been picked up. Only Maya, Braden, Luca and Gemilla remained. Gregor had called to warn her that he would be late. Mark had called, too, to see how Braden was doing. Mark was due at any moment. As soon as he and Braden left, Alex would walk the three cousins to Yetta's where they'd have dinner and hang out until their parents showed up.

"Mom's watching Maya tonight so Rob and I can go out on a date. Our first since the wedding, I swear," Kate had told her that morning. "She's making soup and said you're invited."

Alex tidied up her desk then walked to the table where the children were sitting. Maya and Gemilla were coloring. Luca was scrunched down, his attention focused on a hand-held game. Braden appeared to be doing nothing, but as she watched him, she saw that he was actually paying close attention to the other children.

As if sensing his scrutiny, Maya looked up and smiled at him. "You're a nice boy," she said. "I like you."

Braden's gaze dropped.

Gemilla picked up a fat red crayon. She was rounder and less petite than Maya. Her wispy hair was just as dark, but cut short to give her a pixie look. Alex knew that Gemilla secretly coveted Maya's long curls.

"I like your hair," Gemilla said.

Maya shook her head to make the pigtails that were resting slightly cock-eyed atop her head dance. "Rob did it for me. He bought me a book on braids, but that didn't work out."

"How come?" Gemilla asked.

"Because my hair has a mind of its own," Maya said, in a put-upon tone that probably parroted her stepfather's.

"Oh," Gemilla said.

"Well, braids or not, I think this is a very attractive style for you, and I give Rob credit for trying," Alex put in, as she pulled up a chair.

Maya look at her aunt. "That's what Mommy said, too. I saw a picture of you when your hair was long like mine. Why did you cut it off?"

Not by choice, Alex thought. A reaction to one of the antibiotics they'd given her in the hospital had made her hair turn brittle and start to break. Plus, she'd been too weak to brush and care for the waist-length locks, so she'd let her mother cut it.

"Because I was ready for a change. Sometimes change can be a bit scary, even though it turns out well," Alex said, recalling her sister's concern about Maya's resistance to going to a new school.

Maya reached up and brushed a wavy black lock out of Alex's eyes. "You're still very beautiful, even without my kind of hair," the little girl said.

"She's right," a deep, masculine voice said.

Everyone at the table, including Alex, startled. She couldn't believe Mark had slipped in without her hearing.

What kind of secure environment was this for his child? She jumped to her feet. "How did you—?"

"It's a cop thing. The door was unlocked and you were all so intent…" He shrugged. "Sorry if I scared you."

Alex struggled to find her inner balance. She'd never be able to let Braden stay if she acted like a teenage girl in love every time his father showed up. "No problem. I just don't want you to think our security is lax. Strangers can't just waltz in here and take a child."

He nodded. "I'm sure it's very safe. But if you ever want me to double-check, just ask. In fact, I read in your hand-book that you give a discount to parents who volunteer, and I'm all for saving money. If there's anything I can do after hours, let me know."

After hours. The offer was tempting. Last night, she'd spent three hours studying potential sperm donors and none seemed as qualified as Mark. Of course, that wasn't what he had in mind.

"Um, thanks. I'll think about it." To Braden, she said, "Would you like me to help you get your coat and backpack?"

"I'll help him," Maya said. "Come on, Braden."

The little boy stood up and followed her toward the cloakroom without hesitation.

"Wow," Mark said softly. "I've never seen him actually interact with another kid before. That's great, Alex. How'd he do with his flash cards?"

She'd already picked them up and put them in the box they'd come in. "Not so good. He wasn't interested, and I didn't want to push him. Not on his first day in a new place. But we'll work out a routine soon enough. How was your day?"

His handsome face changed. Still handsome, but not as

friendly and open. "Something's come up at work. Not good. I'll keep you posted as it unfolds. I might actually need…well, I'll talk to you more when I know something."

She wondered if he was being given a different shift and might need her to watch Braden on weekends. On rare occasions she babysat Gregor's kids. And Maya was always welcome to stay. But Alex had a rule about not watching her students outside of regular business hours.

Braden and Maya returned a moment later, and Alex introduced Mark to the children. "Gemilla, Maya, Luca, this is Mr. Gaylord. He's an investigator with the fire department. He finds people who set fires on purpose."

She made sure Luca shook hands with Mark.

To Mark, she said, "Sometimes, parents come in and talk to the children about their jobs. Would you be interested?"

"Maybe," he said. "We'll see."

Alex was a little surprised by his vacillation. Mark had always been enthusiastic about his work, but she let the matter go as he helped his son into his coat.

Maya took Alex's hand as they followed father and son to the door. "Night, Braden. See you tomorrow."

"Bye, Braden. Sweet dreams." Maya waved her free hand.

Both Gaylords seemed anxious to leave, so Alex closed the door behind them and looked at her niece. "Why did you wish him sweet dreams? He won't be going to bed for hours yet."

"Because he's sad, and sometimes bad things happen in his dreams."

"Did he tell you that?"

Maya shook her head. "Auntie, he doesn't talk."

The simple truth made Alex blush. "I know. Then how…?" She didn't finish the question. The family generally accepted the fact that Maya knew things. She was bright and intuitive and seemed to read people the way the average person read a newspaper. But still… "He has bad dreams?"

Maya nodded.

"Does his dad know?"

The little girl shrugged. "You could ask him. *He* can talk."

Another simple truth. And Alex would. Tomorrow.

MARK DROVE STRAIGHT from Alex's to Zeke's. The man's older three-bedroom home was only a few miles from the Radonovic compound. Handy for a man who was doing his best to date the matriarch of the clan, Mark noted.

He tapped his horn as he pulled into the driveway. Turning to look at Braden in the backseat, Mark said, "There's a Happy Meal in the bag on the floor. You can dig in while Zeke and I talk. We're going to be right outside the car, okay?"

To his surprise, Braden acknowledged his father's question with a nod before leaning down to pick up the paper bag adorned with golden arches. Mark felt guilty about how often he fed his son fast food. He wasn't a great cook, but he could do better than this—if today hadn't been a slide into hell.

A flash of movement alerted him to Zeke's presence and he got out of the car. The wind was cold. He wished he had the wool scarf Alex had given him their first Christmas together. Too bad his jealous ex-wife had burned it in the fireplace of the apartment they'd moved into after their quickie wedding.

"Thanks for meeting me," he said, shaking Zeke's hand.

Zeke hadn't changed in all the years Mark had known him. A little more gray, of course, but still as lean and unflappable as ever. "No problem. I'm headed back the way you just came as soon as we're done here. So, what's going on?"

Mark groaned. "Hell, I thought you could tell me. All I'm getting from Rubio is that I'm a person of interest." Reuben Rubio was the head of Mark's department. "And that Internal Affairs is looking into the case."

"I have a buddy in I.A. I'll give him a call. You don't know anything about this supposed bomb?"

Mark shook his head. "First I heard about the fire was when Tracey's neighbor called and said Tracey's mom was there and she planned to take Braden." Mark had rushed over and had arrived before Braden's grandmother was done looting Tracey's apartment, but the argument that had ensued had left Braden terrified and borderline hysterical. Apparently, someone had told the little boy his mother was never coming back for him.

"Tracey's mother pretty well cleaned out the place before I even realized she had a key. Was Tracey using? I don't know. She never sounded like it when we talked on the phone, but you know how good she was about covering up."

"Did you ask the mother?"

Mark laughed, his tone bitter. "Odessa would never say anything that might help clear me. She probably thinks if I take the fall for Tracey's death, she'll get custody of Braden." *Over my dead body,* he silently added.

Mark blamed Tracey's mother for the majority of her daughter's problems. A selfish, scheming, manipulative scam artist, Odessa Mapes had used Tracey any way that benefited Odessa—right down to letting a "professional" photographer shoot pictures of the little girl nude. "It's not like I let a bunch of perverts touch her," Odessa had once said, defending her actions.

Zeke pulled a small notebook from the vest pocket of his jacket and scribbled something. "You probably could have looked at the file before this accusation. Now, you're persona non grata where anything about your wife is concerned, so my advice is do your job and let the investigators do theirs."

Mark nodded. He believed in justice, but he also knew that valuable clues could be lost over months. This case hadn't initially been investigated as a homicide. If they reopened it now, the opportunity to prove his innocence might be harder to come by.

ALEX WASN'T IN THE MOOD for a family dinner, but getting out of her mother's kitchen was never easy. Roms liked to eat. And Yetta, like most Romani mothers, loved to feed people.

"It's a new recipe. Jo gave it to me. You have to try a bowl," Yetta said as she helped Maya and Gemilla hang up their jackets. Luca had already disappeared into the living room. Alex could hear the sound of the television come on.

"Zeke's joining us," her mother added.

Zeke. Her mother's undeclared beau. Also the man who probably knew Mark best. Alex had heard about Zeke Martini long before she'd ever met him. Mark had called him his mentor. She couldn't believe she'd blanked out the connection between Zeke and Mark for so long. In the months that Zeke had been involved in her family's affairs, he and Alex had never once spoken of Mark. Proof, she'd hoped, that she'd moved on where Mark was concerned.

"Okay. One bowl of soup. It'll save messing up my kitchen." Which was a lie, of course. Although she had every intention of eating healthy balanced meals to help prepare her body for pregnancy, the truth was by the end of the day she didn't care whether she ate or not. Which was another reason she no longer resembled her namesake, the hippo.

Zeke showed up fifteen minutes later. Alex watched the silver-haired cop enter the room after a light knock. Her mother's face lit up when she saw him, and she even gave a girlish giggle to his peck on her cheek.

Alex was glad to see her mother reengaged in life. She would always miss her father, but life was moving along. Her mother had a right to be happy, to feel loved and desired. So did Alex, although she'd pretty much given up on the desire part. But love…yes, a baby to love. That was a good thing.

"How's Mark's little boy doing, Alex?" Zeke asked after everyone was settled around the table.

The question surprised her. Zeke usually watched and observed, but he rarely asked direct questions of her or her sisters. "Hard to say. Today was his first day. But he seemed pretty comfortable. Didn't you think so, Luca?"

The boy shrugged. "He doesn't talk. So who knows?"

Knowing Luca's antipathy for law enforcement, Alex had been worried about how he'd do at the same table as Zeke. So far, so good, she thought, taking a spoonful of soup. A mélange of flavors that included jalapeño exploded in her mouth.

"Wow, this is great, Mom."

"Sweet-potato bisque with Portuguese sausage and peppers," Yetta said. "I made the children's portion without the hot peppers."

Everyone ate in a companionable silence until Maya said, "Braden's daddy likes you, Aunt Alex."

Alex's spoon froze partway to her lips. She glanced around, hoping no one else had heard Maya's declaration.

No such luck, she decided seeing her mother and Zeke exchange a look.

She finished her spoonful then said, "Braden's father and I used to be good friends. But then he married Braden's mommy, and we didn't see each other for a long time. Now Mr. Gaylord is my client. Do you know that word?"

Maya nodded. "It means boyfriend."

Alex's jaw dropped. "No, it doesn't. A client is a person who does business with you."

"Mommy was Daddy Rob's client, and now they're married."

Well, that was true. At one time, Kate had retained Rob to handle her opposition to her ex-husband's custody claim.

Alex heard a snicker. From her mother. She gave Yetta a stern look then told Maya, "That was different. Mark… Mr. Gaylord…and I aren't getting married."

Maya cocked her head and smiled in a way that made Alex's heart lift and fall peculiarly. "Okay, Aunt Alex, if you say so, but he does like you. So does Braden."

"Honey, I know you're very good at guessing what people are thinking, but since Braden doesn't speak, you can't say for sure what he feels." *And we aren't even going to get into what Mark thinks or feels.*

Maya heaved a sigh. "When we were in Cubbyland, we talked with our eyes. He says you're sad. I told him he was silly. You laugh and sing all the time. He said it's okay. He likes sad people because he's sad, too."

"Why is he sad?" Yetta asked.

Maya shrugged. "Not sure. I'm done. Can I have a cookie now, Grandma?"

Alex looked at her mother. She didn't like the concern

she read in Yetta's eyes. *Oh, great,* she thought, *just what I need—my family thinking I'm on the verge of depression.*

"I wanna cookie, too," Gemilla said. "I don't like soup. Where's my daddy?"

Fortunately, the children's needs took precedence over the perceived ennui of an aunt, but Alex knew she'd hear about this later. Hopefully, much later.

Chapter Five

Alex couldn't believe how fast the week had flown by. She'd lived through four afternoons with Braden and five meetings with Braden's father. She deserved a drink. Too bad she was abstaining from alcohol. And caffeine.

She'd finally broken down and asked Liz if there was any kind of herbal teas or supplements that were recommended for a woman who was planning on getting pregnant after several years of taking birth-control pills.

Of course, Alex had made it clear that the inquiry was on behalf of one of the Dancing Hippo mothers who desperately wanted a second child. In the past, Liz might have questioned Alex a bit more intently and discovered the truth behind the request, but these days Liz was too preoccupied to look deeper.

In fact, all three of her sisters were pretty wrapped up in their own lives. For the first time in…maybe forever, Alex felt freed from her family's intense, albeit loving, scrutiny. The independence was both exhilarating and daunting.

Did she really dare go through with such a huge, life-altering decision without talking to her sisters first? Now would be the perfect time to bring up the subject, she thought, as she watched Liz loop a strand of mini lights around the corner post of the fence.

Today was Saturday. Grace had arrived on a red-eye flight from Detroit Thursday night. She'd attended some sort of legal hearing yesterday and, now, she and Liz were helping Alex put up outside decorations around the Hippo while waiting for Paul to return with Lydia and Reezira.

Alex couldn't decide who was more excited about the move—Liz and her hubby-to-be or their two Romanian boarders.

"Not those, Grace," Alex said, pointing to the strand of old-fashioned lights her sister was holding. "I'm giving Mom all the red ones."

"Red? Seriously?" Grace appeared shocked.

"I know. She's used blue and white for as long as I can remember, but she told me yesterday she was ready for a change."

"Uh-oh," Grace said. "I wonder what that means. Do you suppose it's Mom's subtle way of telling us she's serious about Zeke?"

Alex had known that was coming. "I raised that question, and she said—and I quote, 'Tell Grace that red lights mean I want red lights. Period.'"

"She didn't say that."

"Absolute truth."

Grace tossed her head in a Grace fashion and crossed her arms. "Fine. If you say so, but something fishy is going on around here. I can sense it. Someone has a secret."

Alex turned back to the holly bush she was draping with lights. Alex had learned never to underestimate her youngest sister's clairvoyant abilities. All four Radonovic sisters had certain sensibilities, but Grace was by far the most open about hers.

Liz let out a low groan. "Okay, I give. It's me."

Alex looked over her shoulder. Liz had taken off her gardening gloves and was resting her butt against the Dancing Hippo sign, which Alex had decorated the week before. "It is?"

"Uh-huh. I…I'm going to be a mother."

Alex nearly fell off the child-size step she was balancing on. "What? When? You aren't even married yet." Which she realized was a ridiculously hypocritical thing to say when she was secretly planning on conceiving without a husband anywhere in sight.

"We will be by the time the baby comes. This process could take a year or more."

"Huh?"

"Paul and I are going to adopt a child from India." She held up a hand before either of her sisters could say anything. "No. Not Prisha," she quickly added. Prisha was the handicapped little girl Liz had met in her travels to an Indian ashram. That adoption had fallen through when Prisha's birth mother had returned for her daughter. "She's doing very well with her mother, and I couldn't be happier for them both. But Paul knew how much Prisha meant to me, and he was determined to help me find another child."

Alex looked at Grace, who was smiling. "You've found one, haven't you?" she asked.

"We think so," Liz said, stressing the word *think*. "Paul has a friend in the State Department who is helping to expedite the paperwork, but anything could happen so we're not getting our hopes up too high."

"What if you have a child of your own before then?"

Liz shrugged. "Mom had two kids fifteen months apart. Neither Alex nor I turned out too neurotic. Wait. I take that back. The jury's still out on Alex. Did Mom tell you what she did?"

Grace walked to where Liz was standing. "No. What?"

"She accepted Mark Gaylord's son into her after-school program."

"No way."

They both looked at her, and Alex felt an uncharacteristic desire to run and hide. "He's a sad little boy with a speech impediment. Stop reading more into this than there is. I provide a service that Mark desperately needs."

"He must have been desperate to come to you," Grace said.

"Thanks a lot."

She waved her hand. "Oh, pooh, you know what I meant. Everyone knows you're a fabulous teacher. I'm surprised he didn't bring his kid here years ago. What does his wife say about this?"

Alex picked up the loose end of her light cord and plugged it into the extension cord she'd bought at Lowe's. Since it was only noon, the little lights barely glowed, but she was satisfied the strand worked.

Turning around to face Grace, she said, "Tracey died last March. Some sort of accident. I meant to search online for it, but I've been a little shorthanded…as Liz knows."

Liz nodded. "I don't mind helping out, Alex. Working with the kids gives me a chance to see what it's going to be like after I have my own. You can call me anytime."

Alex appreciated the offer, even though she still hadn't quite decided how she felt about Liz's declaration that she was going to be a mother. She could certainly empathize with Liz's desire to have a child but wasn't clear on why Liz was so intent on adopting.

Suddenly a thought struck her. "Oh, no, Liz," she said reaching out. "This isn't a result of what happened to you in Bosnia, is it? The rape?"

Liz made a face. "No. As far as I know I *can* have children, and like I said, Paul and I hope to someday. But this is something I want to do."

Alex understood. Some dreams were impossible to give up entirely.

Grace hugged Liz and motioned Alex to join in. "Come on, Alex. Group hugs are something I don't get living in Detroit. I know Nikolai and I are meant for each other, and I've never been happier, but, darn, I miss you guys."

Alex wrapped her arms around her sisters. She felt for Grace. Sometimes her family could be overbearing and nosy, but most of the time they were a source of comfort and security. "We miss you, too, Gracie."

When they stepped back, Grace was sniffling. She pulled off her glove and grabbed a tissue from the pocket of her jean jacket. "Am I spoiled or what?" She didn't wait for an answer, adding, "I try to tell myself to suck it up and get more involved in the Detroit world, but it's so darn cold I can barely make myself take Rip for a walk." Rip was Nick's dog. "And Nick's parents just left on a cruise, so now I'm really alone."

"So they're not selling their house and moving?" Alex asked.

"They took it off the market. I don't think they know what they want to do. Right now, Jurek is house-sitting for them."

Jurek was Nick's birth father.

"Will they still be traveling over Christmas?" Liz asked.

"No. They plan to spend Christmas with Nick's sister, and then fly down here for New Year's Eve. We'll go back together." The last came out as a tearful hiccup, which made Liz and Alex look at each other and laugh.

"She really is spoiled," Liz said.

"Pathetic," Alex agreed.

Grace stuck out her tongue then skipped back to the fence to finish her lighting job. "Not my fault. I grew up believing I was a Gypsy princess, and now my husband-to-be treats me like a queen."

Liz groaned. "Braggart. But speaking of fiancés, there's mine. Sorry, Alex, I have to run. Once we get the girls unpacked, Paul and I are going to Romantique for dinner. I swear he can't get enough of that place, which is fine with me because one, I hate to cook and two, I have to deliver some tea."

Alex watched Liz dash across the street and disappear into their mother's home. The lightness in her step made Alex smile.

"She's like a different person, isn't she?"

Alex turned to find Grace right beside her. She hadn't heard her walk up. "Um…yeah. They say love will do that to a person."

"It's true. I remember thinking the same thing about you when you fell in love with Mark."

"Really? Weren't you living in Colorado then?"

Grace nodded. "Yup, and every time I came home, it was like watching a documentary on falling in love. You and Mark were so perfect for each other. You looked great together and you were obviously madly in love." She shrugged. "You two set the bar really high, let me tell you.

Which in no way explains how I managed to fall for such a loser the first time around—before I met Nikolai."

Alex smiled. Grace was always quick to poke fun at herself. She was now even able to joke about her relationship with a gorgeous ski bum who'd cheated on her. Which, ironically, was not unlike Alex's situation.

"Getting back to Mark and his kid," Grace said a second later, "are you sure this is a good idea? Isn't seeing him on a daily basis opening yourself up to old heartache?"

Alex bent over to pick up the spare lights and put them in the plastic storage box. "I don't think so. What happened between us was a long time ago. I've dated quite a few men since Mark and—"

"None of them matched up to him."

True, but not the point she was trying to make. "And I've decided that unlike my very lucky sisters, there is no Mr. Right looking for me."

Grace made a yelp as if Alex had kicked her. "No, don't say that. You know there's a man for you. Your prophecy says…" Alex could see Grace trying to recall the exact wording of the prediction their mother had made when Alex was a little girl.

A child's laughter can heal a wounded heart, if first you heal the child.

Back then, Alex had believed it.

She'd embraced the idea that Mark was the child who'd needed healing. From the first time he'd talked about his relationship with his father, she'd understood that beneath his tough-cop bravado was a wounded little boy. She'd been convinced her love had helped heal his torment. They'd laughed and loved and been so happy together.

Until…Braden.

"Let's drop it, Grace, okay? I still have a lot of things to get done around here, and didn't I hear you were helping out at the restaurant tonight?"

Grace sighed. "Yeah. For old times' sake. I miss Romantique, too, but don't tell Nikolai. He'd feel badly. He tries to be my everything, and he is—in certain ways," she said with a playful grin, "but I guess a part of me will always be here with my family."

Alex understood. "I used to feel embarrassed because I was over thirty and living across the street from my parents. But not anymore. This works for me. I love my family, and the proximity will be even more important when I—" She stopped herself just in time.

"When you…?"

Damn. She had to blow it with Grace. "When I'm old and decrepit. What else?"

Grace had a suspicious look in her eyes, but before she could say anything, a horn sounded and Kate pulled into the cul-de-sac. "I have warm Danish," she called. "My mother-in-law's gift to Grace, but we all get to share."

"Danish? I love Jo's Danish," Grace exclaimed, doing a little dance. "It may mean ordering my wedding dress one size larger, but Nikolai says he likes a little meat on my bones."

Mark used to tell Alex that, too. Her weight had never bothered her. Even in her teens, when all her friends were on crash diets, Alex had felt comfortable in her body. If a guy wasn't interested in a size-sixteen girl, then his loss, she'd figured.

Grace paused at the gate. "Aren't you coming?"

"Go ahead and start without me. I have to put these boxes in the shed."

"Better hurry. I'm not promising to save you anything."

Alex laughed and picked up the mostly empty box. She was taking Liz's advice and sticking to a healthy diet. No extra fats or refined sugar. But she didn't intend to tell her family that. Not yet.

MARK WAS SORTING LAUNDRY when the call came. As usual, he checked the number before answering. He recognized the caller. His heart rate increased. *Take it or not?*

"Oh, hell, she'll track me down if I don't," he mumbled. "What do you want, Odessa?"

"A civil greeting, for one thing," the woman replied.

Mark didn't say a word.

"You're a hard, unforgiving man, Mark Gaylord. Why my daughter worked so hard to snag you is beyond me."

Snag. Great word. Made him feel like a fish scooped out of the river.

"Make your point, Odessa. I don't have time for chitchat."

"Chitchat? Is that what you call it when I haven't seen my baby grandson in two months and every time I call, you make some lame excuse about his mental state? I'm sick of the runaround, Mark. I want to see my grandson. Now. Today."

"Impossible. I just got him settled in a new afterschool program. He's doing better and I don't want you upsetting him."

"Me? I'm not the one who killed his mother—your wife."

The words sounded hauntingly like the rumor being whispered around the fire house. "Tracey and I were divorced, Odessa. You know that. I had nothing to do with what happened to her, and I resent the—"

"You'll resent a lot more once they put you in jail for murder, won't you?"

Mark's hands stilled on the pile of cold, damp jeans that he was preparing to put in the dryer. The reopening of Tracey's case wasn't common knowledge. No charges had been filed. How had she heard about it? "What are you talking about?"

"You know," she said with a cackle. "Tracey still has friends in the department. Finally, the truth will come out and vindicate my poor baby girl. You sent her to that evil place. You tricked her into going there, then you set up some sort of bomb and had it rigged to blow when she went in. You did it, Mark. You killed my daughter."

The words echoed in Mark's head even as he hung up the receiver. Feeling light-headed, he turned around, intending to get a glass of water to calm his nerves.

Braden was standing a few feet away. Had he heard his grandmother's charges? How could he not? The woman had been practically shrieking. None of the specialists had ever said Braden's hearing was compromised, only his ability to speak.

On impulse, Mark bent over and picked up his son. He set him on the dryer so they were just about eye to eye. "That was your Grandma Odessa. She's never really forgiven me for marrying your mother. I can't do anything about that, but I don't have to listen to her. If she calls back, I won't pick up the phone. Are we clear on that?"

Braden nodded.

Mark took a breath and let it go. The room smelled like fabric softener and warm moist heat. But the cozy safety had been violated, and Mark only knew one way to escape his fears—outrun them. "How 'bout we take the bikes and get out of here?"

Braden nodded again, with volume.

"Cool. Go change your clothes. A warm sweatshirt, for sure. I have one quick call to make." Probably a mistake. A big mistake. But…he punched in the number he'd already memorized. She picked up on the third ring. She sounded breathless, as if she'd run in from outdoors.

"Alex, it's Mark. I wanted to share my good news. Braden has nodded affirmative. Twice. And the second time was almost loud."

Her laugh made him feel better about the call. He'd known she would understand. This was progress, of sorts, and she'd undoubtedly played a part in making that happen. Braden had been sleeping better since he'd started going to the Hippo. He still had nightmares, but they didn't seem as bad. So she deserved to share in the rewards, right?

"Bray and I are going for a bike ride. Out in Red Rock Canyon. Do you want to go with us?"

She didn't answer right away. He could almost hear all the reasons not to go racing through her head, but he waited. Hopeful. Nervous. Ridiculous.

"I shouldn't. I still have so much to do around here, but I haven't been to Red Rocks since before my dad's first stroke. He used to take us girls hiking there all the time. I'm tempted—even if I won't be able to keep up with two guys on bikes."

"Don't worry. We'll let you set the pace. Can you be ready in twenty minutes?"

"Um…sure. Why not?"

Chapter Six

"'Why not?' Did I honestly say 'why not?'" Alex muttered hanging up the phone. "Good grief. Let me call one of my sisters and get a list of all the reasons why I have no business going anywhere with Mark. Starting with the fact that he's the low-down rotten bastard who cheated on me."

But much as she wanted to hate him, she didn't.

"What's wrong with me? Hormones?" She looked at her belly as if expecting to see some visual proof of the menacing little secretions pulsing through her body.

She unclenched her grip on a red-and-white felt Santa decoration and sighed. The truth was each December she found it harder and harder to muster the appropriate level of holiday spirit necessary for working with children. As much as she loved watching her charges discover the marvels of the season, something was missing. She wanted to shop, decorate and bake for her own family.

She tossed Santa back into the box and patted her tummy. "Maybe next year," she murmured. "But, now, I'm playing hooky. Liz said exercise was a must for preprenatal mothers, so…" She hurried into her room to change clothes. A couple of layers. Extra socks. Sunscreen—even the winter sun could burn in this part of the country. Stretchy workout gloves that she'd bought last year when Grace had been on a self-improvement kick.

Her bike was in the shed at the back of the lot. She kept her fingers crossed that the tires weren't flat. "A little low, but not bad," she said as she wheeled it into the yard. She used a rag to dust off the seat then pushed it through the side gate to the covered carport where her compact sedan sat. She didn't have a bike lock, and even in a nice neighborhood like this, it wasn't a good idea to leave things sitting around.

"Water bottle, lip gloss, energy bars…" She was making a list of items to retrieve from her kitchen when she spotted Luca whiz past on his bicycle.

Putting two fingers between her lips, she whistled. The little boy jammed on the brakes and turned around. "Hey."

She motioned him closer. "Would you do me a favor and watch my bike while I run inside. I need a couple of things."

"Sure. Where are you riding to?"

Can I come?

He didn't say the words out loud, but Alex heard them in his tone. Poor kid. Forced to grow up too fast when his mother got sick and his dad had to do everything.

"Braden and his dad are taking me with them. I don't know what kind of vehicle Mr. Gaylord drives. If there's room for a fourth bike, do you want to come with us?"

His shoulders lifted and fell in a careless gesture, but Alex could see the interest in his eyes. She sincerely hoped Mark wouldn't mind having another child along.

She'd just barely returned with her sack of goodies when a Dodge pickup truck pulled into her driveway. The four-door vehicle looked plenty large to accommodate another bike. *Please say yes, Mark,* she thought, hurrying to meet him.

"Hi, Mark. You're fast. I think my tires could use a little air, but my cousin, Gregor, has a pump, doesn't he, Luca?"

Luca nodded.

Mark greeted Alex and smiled a greeting at the boy beside her. "Great. I've been meaning to buy one, but we don't ride as often as we should and it seems to slip my mind between times." He paused and then said, "Luca, would you like to come with us? If your dad says it's okay, of course."

Alex's heart did a trippy little dance that reminded her of when she and Mark had first met. He always did the right thing when it came to kids.

"Okay," Luca said. "He won't care. He's doing laundry and watching football."

Mark took the knapsack Alex was carrying and wheeled her bike toward the truck. "We should hurry. It gets dark so early this time of year."

Alex and Braden followed Mark and Luca across the street. Sure enough, Gregor was happy to see his son doing something constructive, although he did pull Alex aside while Luca and Mark retrieved the hand pump and said, "Is that who I think it is?"

She nodded. "Probably. Mark and I were engaged once. A long time ago."

"That's what I thought. And now…"

"Now his son…" she put a hand on Braden's shoulder "…is coming to the Hippo after school. He and Luca have been getting to know each other." Not completely true. Neither boy had made any effort to spend time together, but they crossed paths every day. "This will be fun for both of them."

"Sure," Greg said. "Better than having him moping

around here all day. He could have gone to the ranch with Dad and Gemilla, but he didn't have his homework done."

Greg's father, Alex's uncle, Claude, had moved in with Greg's brother a few months earlier. All of the children loved spending time at the small ranch west of town where Claude raised Shetland ponies. "But I checked Luca's homework last night. He said he only had math, and he completed that before I let him play his video game."

Mark and Luca had returned. Luca looked down as his father explained, "Extra-credit reading. He had a book report to write, and he just finished it a few minutes ago. Right, son?"

Luca nodded.

Alex understood. Her cousin's son was as smart as a whip, but he had a slight learning disability that made reading difficult for him. He could do the work, but it took time, and like most kids his age preferred play over schoolwork.

"Great. You got it done. That means you can go with us. Shall we?"

Mark quickly secured Luca's bike beside Alex's and they were off, heading west. The first leg of their journey wound past high-end housing developments and golf courses that had a Southern California look to them. But once the houses stopped, the desert took over.

"So close and yet I get out here so seldom," Alex said with a sigh. She was enjoying the view from the comfortable passenger seat of the four-wheel-drive truck.

"I know what you mean. I bought an annual pass to Red Rocks thinking that would make me come out more often. Just hasn't happened, has it, Bray? When was the last time we were here?"

The lack of a reply seemed to change the tension level in the cab of the truck. Country music was playing on the satellite radio, but the volume wasn't loud enough to fill the void.

Alex turned in her seat so she could see the two boys in the back. "How 'bout a game of roadside hangman?"

The word *game* made Luca sit up straighter and look around. A natural competitor, he seemed intent on being the first one to spot something that started with the letter *H*.

"Hole," he said, pointing to a divot scooped out of a hill-side by a big yellow backhoe.

"Very good. Let's see who gets the letter *A*."

Nobody spoke for a minute then Mark said, "Alligator."

Alex, Luca and Braden looked at each other dubiously. "Yeah, right," Alex said, speaking for all of them.

"No, seriously. See that hunk of tire on the side of the road? Truck drivers call them gators. Short for alligator."

Alex looked at Braden. "Do we believe him?"

The child nodded.

"Okay," she said with a sigh. "Mark has the second letter. But the next is a toughie—*N*."

She scanned the road ahead and pointed. "Not as hard as I thought. There's the word *Nevada*. On the sign. Right there. You saw it, right?"

Mark groaned. "Yeah, I saw it, but I think that's cheating. What do you guys say?"

She saw the boys look at each other and make some kind of silent agreement. "She can have it," Luca said. "What's next?"

Alex spelled out H-A-N-G… *"G."*

They drove in silence for a few miles then a small voice said, "Gr-green."

Mark's chin turned to look at her, his eyes wide. "Bra-den?" he mouthed.

Alex looked at the boy directly behind his father. "Green? What did you see that's green, Braden? I missed it."

The child looked down as if embarrassed by his outburst.

"That spiky plant back there," Luca supplied pointing over his shoulder. "I can't remember the name. I saw it, too, but I didn't think about the color. That was good, Braden."

Moisture welled up in her eyes and she quickly turned back around. She didn't want to make either child feel awkward. "Excellent," she said, her throat tight. "You guys are really terrific at this game, but I think we should quit now because here's the entrance to the park. We can do the last letters on the way home, okay?"

Besides, any answer now would be an anticlimax. Braden had spoken. But more than that, he'd participated. That was something to shout about.

Not that she did, of course, but fifteen minutes later— once the boys were far enough ahead of her and Mark to be out of earshot—she said, "That was so cool."

"I know, except I almost drove off the road."

"I've noticed him watching more actively all week. He doesn't actually participate in the games the other children are playing, but his gaze lingers, and sometimes he'll lean closer to Maya when she's showing him something. She's pretty much adopted him as her pet project."

"She's a cutie. Looks a lot like her aunt."

Alex blushed, but she was sure the chilly wind had added enough color to her cheeks to cover it. "Maya's mother wants to move her to a preschool that's closer to their new home, but Maya isn't having anything to do with that. She's a very determined little girl." She shrugged. "Which could be a good thing for Braden."

"How do you mean?"

"Well, he's used to having teachers working with him, asking things of him, but Maya is different. She treats him like her equal, even though he never says a word. Most of the time she answers for him, as if she's reading his mind."

Mark swerved slightly. "Can she do that? Read his mind? I mean, she's got the right blood for it."

Alex made a flip-flop motion with her hand. "She's an intuitive little girl, there's no question of that, but we've never seen any real psychic abilities. Not like Grace and Mom."

"Grace?"

She told him the story of Grace's precognition that someone was going to be shot and how she put herself in harm's way to protect Nikolai—her "prince."

"I heard a little bit of that story from Zeke, but he's not exactly a gossip."

"You know he's dating my mother, right?"

"Uh-huh. How does the family feel about that?"

"For the most part, we like him, and we're glad Mom's moving on with her life, but…"

"He's a *gaujo* cop. Like me."

She frowned. Was that bitterness she heard in his use of the word for "non-Romani"? Mark's job had only been part of the reason her father had been so against his marrying Alex. Ernst had worried about what effect Mark's unhappy childhood would have on his ability to be a good husband and father. At the time, Alex had taken Mark's side without reservation, but after their breakup she'd seen that maybe her father had been right.

"Deep down I think Mark knew he could never live up to your expectations, Alex," her father had said, trying to comfort her. "You're better off without him."

Anger and hurt had reinforced that sentiment, and for

years, her private mantra had been: "I'm better off without him." She still believed that. Didn't she?

Alex put the question from her mind. "Actually, Grace is marrying a cop. He's part Rom, but he's not exactly jumping for joy about that. So, I don't think Zeke's bloodline is the problem."

"But you still have reservations. I can sense your hesitation. What don't you like about him? Zeke's a helluva guy. I'd trust him with my life."

"It's not that I don't like him, but he's been single a long time. His children live in another state and he hasn't had a lot to do with them over the years. I'm not sure he's ready for all the…um…*baggage* Mom brings to the equation. Four daughters. One new son-in-law and two more in the wings. Plus the Romani clan, in general. We're a handful."

He chuckled. "That you are, but to be honest, I never felt more included in any group than when we were together. Except where your dad was concerned." He cleared his throat and added, "Regardless, I was real sorry to hear about his passing. The Gypsy King was one of a kind."

She nodded but didn't say anything. She couldn't. She still missed her father more than she could express. And being in Red Rocks was like playing in Ernst's own personal backyard—the memories were everywhere.

"The boys seem to be getting along well," Mark said, nodding with his chin at the two specks ahead of them.

"Fresh air and exercise are like superglue for kids. Bonds them together."

"Even when one doesn't talk?"

"He can ride. Fast. That speaks volumes."

He smiled and looked at her. "I really like you, Alex.

The person you've become. I always knew you'd be an amazing woman—you were when I met you, but now you're even more."

"And less," she teased, poking her belly.

His gaze lingered. "Yes, you've changed in a lot of ways. I have to admit I miss your long hair, but this style suits you—very cheerful and fun."

"Really?" She sat up and dashed her fingers through the wind-tossed locks. "I was going for suave and sexy. Just kidding," she quickly added at his surprised look. "No fuss is the best thing where kids are concerned. Some days, you wind up with paint, modeling clay, sand, frosting *and* glue in your hair. Preschool…it can be a war zone."

"Sounds like it. By the way, I um…might be having some time off in the near future, and I wondered if your parent volunteers include dads?"

"Of course, but since Braden only comes after school, there's not as much opportunity for formal—"

He cut her off. "I didn't mean just the hours that Bray is there. I asked his teacher about helping out in the classroom, and she wasn't wild about the idea. Said the kids get distracted by the presence of a parent—particularly a male parent—in the room. But I'd really like to learn more about working with kids. I think it would be good for both of us— me and Braden."

Both of us. Alex didn't want to admit that her first thought had been her and Mark.

"Well, I can always use the help, but I've never had a parent offer to give up his vacation to work at my school."

Mark looked ahead to make sure Braden wasn't close enough to hear, then he told her, "I'm not talking vacation. They've reopened the case on Tracey's death. A new source has come forth who claims I rigged a bomb that killed Tracey."

"No," she cried with a conviction that did his heart good. "That's impossible. You wouldn't do something like that."

"The fire was intense—meth labs in and of themselves are extremely volatile. I wasn't involved in the investigation—in fact, I was off on six weeks of personal leave while I took care of Braden, but I heard through the grapevine that the original investigation failed to turn up any kind of trigger device. This allegation wouldn't have been taken seriously if the guy hadn't named names. Mine. And Tracey's."

"That's really upsetting. Just what you and Braden don't need, right? Well, if you have some time off and need to fill it, you're more than welcome at the Hippo. And if there's anything I can do where Braden is concerned…"

"You could adopt him," Mark tossed out. The thought hadn't entered his mind until his ex-mother-in-law had called that morning. He was confident that his innocence would come out in the investigation, but he'd been a cop before he was an arson investigator and he knew that sometimes the facts could lead to the wrong conclusion. If, by any chance, he was arrested, he had to have a plan set up that kept Braden from falling into Odessa's hands.

Alex turned the handles of her bike too sharply and accidentally bumped into Mark's front tire. He overcompensated and they nearly crashed, but his quick reflexes help bring them both to a stop without serious damage.

"Sorry," she said. "I must have misunderstood. I thought you said I should…" Obviously she couldn't bring herself to say the word.

"Adopt. I shouldn't have just blurted that out. I apologize. That was stupid."

"Explain what you mean then I'll tell you if it was stupid or not."

"Later. We should catch up with the boys."

Alex gave him a stern look. "Now. They'll realize we're not behind them and come back. I want to know what you meant. Is there a chance you're going to jail?"

"No. Well, I'm a suspect, but I'm not a murderer, and I don't expect to be arrested. But anything could happen. And I just realized this morning that I haven't made any plans for Braden, if something happened to me."

Her frown didn't abate in the least. "Doesn't Tracey have a mother in the area?"

"Yes, but he'd be better off taking his chances as a ward of the court than with Odessa."

She swallowed. "Do you say that because you dislike her or because she's…?"

"A whack job. She screwed up her daughter, and I'm not about to let her get her hands on my son. I don't trust her, Alex. You, I trust. You would always look after him with Braden's best interests at heart. Of course, I have no right to ask you this, but you'd be my first choice as my son's guardian. If it comes down to that."

Chapter Seven

If it comes down to that.

The phrase was haunting Alex. She'd managed to keep from overreacting—well, except for nearly causing them to crash, when Mark had first made his suggestion. But, the idea had bounced around in her head the rest of the afternoon, and had even followed her home as she'd put away her bike, heated up some leftover soup and settled into a hot bath.

She'd agreed to let Mark's son come to her after-school program. How could he possibly have made such a quantum leap in their relationship?

I like you, he'd said.

Much as she hated to admit it, she liked him, too. A part of her still wanted to fan the flame of her outrage, but too much time had passed to nurse that fire to life. She'd changed. Maybe she'd seen too many instances where hurt feelings led to furious battles that left wounded children struggling to pick up the pieces. Children like Braden.

Mark truly seemed to have become the man she'd always thought he was capable of being—smart, kind, generous of spirit. Except where his mother-in-law was concerned. Alex had been chilled by the look in Mark's eyes when he'd spoken of Tracey's mother.

Alex vaguely remembered hearing some mention of his partner's troubled home life when Mark had been first assigned to work with the female rookie. One comment that stuck in Alex's brain was Mark saying, "Tracey's childhood makes mine look like an episode of *Leave It To Beaver*."

From the little he'd told Alex, she'd gotten a pretty strong impression of his bleak childhood. Mark had gotten out as soon as possible and made a life for himself that didn't include booze.

Tracey may have shared a similar past, but she hadn't been able to make that leap to a healthier lifestyle. Instead, she'd developed a reputation as a partier, apparently following in her mother's footsteps.

But none of that was Alex's problem. Right?

She sank down a little lower in her oversize tub. Her oasis. One that didn't normally include a phone. But Alex was expecting Grace's call, so she'd carried her portable phone into the steamy room and set it on the counter beside the bath.

She moved her knees to send a wave of bubbles crashing over her collarbones. *Heavenly.* She wouldn't think about today. About Braden. Or Mark.

The phone rang.

Keeping her eyes closed, she reached out and pushed the button to talk. "Are you done already? I was sure I had time for a bath."

"Um…you're in the tub?"

Mark. Alex's eyes flew open and she sat up, sending a second wave crashing over her toes.

"If I remember correctly, that's a two-person tub."

"Uh…I…was expecting Grace to call. We're going for

ice cream after she gets done hostessing at Romantique. I thought a hot soak would do my aching muscles some good." She was talking too fast. Saying too much. She didn't owe him any explanations. "Why did you call?"

"To apologize. I shouldn't have said anything today about my situation. This isn't your problem, and I'm sorry for laying my fears on your doorstep. I was mostly thinking out loud. Worst-case scenarios and all that. Braden's grandmother called earlier today, and I overreacted."

But that was part of the problem, she thought. Mark didn't overreact. He'd grown up under the thumb of a man who made tearing the newspaper a major crime. Mark rarely said something he didn't mean. Which meant…

"I'm not the person you think I am, Mark. I'm a good preschool teacher, but I'm the first to admit that there's a huge difference between teaching and parenting."

His soft chuckle was almost as warm and soothing as the bathwater. "Oh, Alex, you're going to be the world's best mother someday and you know it. Any child would be blessed to have you in his or her life."

She was tempted to tell him about her plan, but she suddenly felt shy and nervous. This was Mark. The man who should have been, could have been, the father of her child. "Parenting skills aside, you do realize that asking me to be Tracey's son's guardian isn't exactly politically correct, don't you?"

"Like I said, I wasn't thinking about the why-nots, only the whys. And the main reason why you'd be my first choice is that you're you. But, I want you to forget about it. I'm not going to assume that the worst will happen. I didn't do anything wrong, and, corny as it sounds, justice will prevail."

She sincerely hoped so.

"Now, about that bath. Are there bubbles?"

She laughed and eased back into the still-warm water. "Yes. Lilac scented. Now, if you'll excuse me—"

"Lots of bubbles? Or patches that might give an observer a glimpse of body parts? I used to love to watch you bathe. You turned soaking into an art form. But my favorite part was when you picked up the bar of soap because I knew that would kill off the bubbles faster."

"You watched me bathe?" She tried to sound outraged, but really was a little turned on.

"Oh…yeah, whenever possible. Remember our apartment? There was a full-length mirror on the outside of the bathroom door. If you left the door open, I had a pretty good view of the tub."

She gulped and moved an island of bubbles over her breasts. "Isn't that against the law?"

His chuckle went low in her belly. She wiggled her hips. "I always figured you knew. Surely, you suspected. I mean, whenever you got out of the tub, I was right there on the bed, ready and willing, if you get my drift."

She remembered. They'd loved each other with the careless passion of the young—believing they'd always have the next day and the next.

"I thought you were just a horny boy."

His bark of laughter made her smile.

"And I thought you were a Gypsy enchantress. It got to the point where all you had to do was turn on the faucet, and I got hard."

The frankness surprised her. And excited her. "Are you hard now?" she asked before she could stop herself.

He didn't answer right away. "Yeah, as a matter of fact,

I am. If I close my eyes, I can see you in the water. Languid, but in a sexy, wanton way."

Her pulse quickened. She could picture him all too clearly, too. Eight years apart, but she remembered just what he looked like naked. Beautiful. Powerful. No one had ever been able to satisfy her the way Mark had.

"If you inhale, your breasts come out of the water, don't they?" he asked, drawing in an audible breath.

Alex looked down through half-open eyes. Her nipples, hard and deep red, pierced the bubbles. "Yes," she whispered.

"And if you lift your hips, just a little—"

Beep.

"Just a little, your dark, wet curls will—"

Beep.

"Damn," he swore. "I hate call-waiting."

Alex started to laugh—a laugh that partly released the sexual tension she had no business feeling. Good grief, she was having phone sex with a client. Which made her sound like a hooker. "Mark, I have to go. This is Grace and you know Grace. She doesn't like to be kept waiting."

"I remember. But, are we okay about what happened today?"

"Sure. Of course. I gotta go. Bye."

Were they really? She wasn't sure. Things were changing between them. Too fast. And she didn't know if that was a good thing or not. Her instincts said, *Not.* But her instincts had been wrong before. Wrong about Mark.

MARK WASN'T SURPRISED TO FIND that he couldn't go to sleep. He was a wreck—restless, wired and horny as hell. That little episode on the phone with Alex had been a huge mistake. He shot a look at his groin. A cold shower had helped, but crawling into his king-size bed with icy sheets and too much room seemed like the final insult to a really crappy day.

There had been good moments—great moments, like hearing his son speak with barely a stutter, but then he'd blown it with Alex. "Gee, Alex, you're a teacher. You're good with kids. Would you like to adopt mine if I get tossed in jail?" he muttered under his breath.

He flipped to his side and punched his pillow. "What a jerk. Not surprising that she'd nearly driven her bike off a cliff."

An exaggeration. Her front wheel had rammed his bike, instead, but she could have turned right and gone over a steep embankment. A bent spoke was nothing compared to a cross-country crash—rocks, cactus and a potential concussion. As his imagination ran with the image, his stomach started to churn.

Tossing back the covers, he jumped out of bed. His flannel pajama bottoms—a new addition to his wardrobe since becoming a full-time dad—rode low on his hips. He walked into the adjoining bath—an apartment-size cubicle not anything like the room he remembered seeing when he and Alex had been house hunting.

"Ooh, Mark, look at the size of that tub. Do you know what we could do with a tub that big?" she'd teased when the Realtor had stepped away. "Oh, baby, let the splashing begin."

He stood at the sink and looked into the mirror. The harsh overhead lights did little to minimize the effects the past few years had had on him. Gray hairs in his sideburns. Lines across his forehead and around his eyes. Usually, he only looked in the mirror to shave. He didn't enjoy seeing evidence of the mistakes he'd made staring back at him.

"You chose to—" he stopped himself from saying the word he didn't want his son repeating "—screw up your life when you slept with Tracey. This is what you have to deal with, so quit whining about all the things that could have been. You could have been sharing that big tub with Alex. You could have been a lot of things, but this is what you are. Get over it."

He filled a little paper cup with lukewarm water and swallowed it in one gulp, cringing at the chlorine taste. He crushed the cup and tossed it into the garbage can beside the toilet with a snap of his wrist. He'd just clicked off the light when he heard a sound that made his knees weak.

His son's mewling cry was usually a precursor to a three-hour ordeal in nightmare land. Unless he could head off the worst of it… He sprinted down the hallway to Braden's room. The door was open; the SpongeBob Square-Pants night-light cast a yellowish glow across the bed and furnishings. The little boy in the bed was already starting to thrash back and forth. His covers were on the floor.

"Braden," Mark called in a low, intense voice. "Braden, listen to me. It's Daddy. I'm here. You're in your room. Everything is fine. You're safe. Do you hear me, son? You're safe. Daddy's here. Daddy loves you. Open your eyes, Bray. Look at me."

Braden opened his mouth instead of his eyes, and a loud, desperate cry of pain filled the room, breaking Mark's heart. There were no words. No explanation. Nothing to lead Mark to the source of his son's terror. And no clue about how to reassure the little boy.

All he could do was repeat his silent vow to make sure Tracey's mother never got her evil hands on his son.

Chapter Eight

"So, I hear you went bike riding with Mark and his son today."

"Gregor is a worse gossip than any woman I know."

Grace laughed and took a sip on her straw, which was buried in a root-beer float. "True. He called Mom's house before your taillights cleared the cul-de-sac."

Alex had expected as much, but, as she'd explained to Grace, she'd gone on group outings with other students and their parents. "No big deal," she said.

"Uh-huh, and the fact that Mark is still a hunk has nothing to do with your decision to spend the day with him and his handicapped son."

"Braden is *not* handicapped," Alex said emphasizing the word *not*. "Lots of young children stutter. And many go through periods where they don't speak. Particularly after a devastating loss or shock."

Grace had a pleased-with-herself look on her face. "Spoken like a mama bear defending her cub."

Alex felt her face heat up. She'd known meeting Grace for ice cream was a bad idea. Especially after her tub episode with Mark. But she'd been too flustered to come up with a good excuse, so she'd gotten dressed and driven to their neighborhood Dairy Queen.

"As I would defend any child in my care," Alex said, trying to rationalize her response. "He's a sweet little boy who lost his mother, and whose dad is playing catch-up in the parenting department. Plus, I think Braden's come to the conclusion that life pretty much sucks and the best way to avoid getting smacked around is to hide behind a wall of silence."

Grace's eyes went big. "You think Mark hits—"

"Of course not," Alex said sharply. "Mark would never abuse a child. He's patient and gentle with Braden. Why would you even suggest such a thing?"

Grace made a slurping sound with her straw and reached for her spoon. "To gauge your reaction."

Alex fought to keep from blushing, but Grace's snicker told her she'd failed.

"Besides, Zeke told Mom that Mark had been in the process of taking Tracey back to court to get full custody of Braden around the time she was killed. Apparently, he found a big, ugly bruise on Braden's arm a few weeks earlier. Tracey blamed it on the babysitter, but Mark suspected Tracey's mom."

Which probably explains why Mark brought up the idea of me caring for Braden if anything happened to him, Alex thought.

"I haven't gotten to know Braden well enough to figure out what's going on in his head, but he's starting to warm up. He let Maya hold his hand on Friday."

"Really? Oh, my, a new generation of love. This is so cool. Have you told Kate? I wonder if Mother's had a prophecy."

Alex took a bite of her frozen-yogurt hot-fudge sundae. Something else she should feel guilty about, but didn't. Not really. Tonight, she was enjoying her sister's company and pigging out on a comforting dose of chocolate while secretly admitting that she wanted to share a bubble bath with a man who was totally wrong for her. Tomorrow she'd repent for her weaknesses—both gluttony and wantonness—but, first, she'd enjoy every indulgent taste…and every delicious fantasy.

THE NOTICE, WHEN IT CAME three days later, was almost anticlimactic, Mark decided, as he packed a few personal items from his desk. He'd been called into his supervisor's office and told to bring another officer up to speed on his current cases.

"I really hate to do this, Mark," Reuben had told him. "You're the best investigator I've got, but this is out of my hands. I did argue to keep you on paid leave, though. I know how hard it is to get by when you have kids."

Mark appreciated the gesture. He sure as hell wasn't rich, and who knew how long this suspension might last? Until they had enough proof to charge somebody, he guessed. He just hoped that arrest warrant wouldn't have his name on it.

Before leaving, he did what was asked of him, made a few calls—including one to Zeke—and then went home. But the walls of his apartment felt colorless, empty and claustrophobic, so he decided to drive around until it was time to pick up Braden.

He only got as far as the Dancing Hippo. Braden wouldn't arrive for another hour, but Alex had said she could always use an extra hand. Feeling foolish, he walked up the sidewalk, but before he reached the handicap ramp, the front door opened and Yetta walked out.

She didn't appear surprised to see him. "Mark, how lovely. I need two strong arms to help me carry some musical instruments that Alexandra stores in my spare room. What incredible timing."

He wasn't sure what to say. He'd always been on good terms with Alex's mother in the past, but surely she regarded him with some antipathy given the way he'd broken her daughter's heart. Before he could ask any questions, she took his arm and turned him in the opposite direction he'd been heading.

"The children are resting, so this works out perfectly. Come along. It'll give us a chance to clear the air."

He swallowed. "I was sorry to hear about your husband."

Yetta was shorter than Alex, petite but not fragile-looking. Her grip on his arm was pretty strong for a woman dressed in a suit and low heels. Her hair was more silver than he remembered, but the pulled-back style looked rather elegant.

"That's very generous of you, considering how mean-spirited Ernst was toward you when you and Alexandra were dating. I swear I never understood how such an intelligent man could close off his mind to certain undeniable truths."

Truths? "You mean the fact I was a cop?"

She smiled. "No. That's just a job. I was referring to the fact that you and Alexandra loved each other and were perfect for each other."

He shook his head. "Not so perfect. I blew it, remember?"

She patted his arm. "Everyone makes mistakes—even Ernst." Her smile dimmed for a moment, before her expression changed to one of resolve. "All of that is in the past. We must carry on and do the best we can with the present, such as it is. So, is this your day off?"

It was tempting to lie, but could one lie to a Gypsy psychic and get away with it? "Not exactly. I'm on temporary suspension while the powers that be decide whether or not I killed my ex-wife and her drug dealer in a fire at a meth lab."

They'd reached the opposite side of the street and were in front of the house where Alex's cousin lived. Yetta dropped her hold on his arm and stared at him a few seconds, then, to his surprise, she hugged him. "What a difficult road you've chosen, dear boy. I'm so sorry. I wish I could say things were going to get better, but…"

Her gaze shifted slightly so she wasn't looking at him directly. Her gaze appeared fixed on something just beyond him—perhaps beyond what normal people could see. He held his breath waiting to see if she'd say more, but after a few seconds, she shook her head and blinked. "We need to hurry. Alexandra hates to be kept waiting."

Mark almost chuckled at the irony of her statement. In some ways, he'd kept her waiting for nearly eight years. Well, not really. Alex had made it clear that she'd moved on where he was concerned. He needed to remember that. His life was a mess. He had even less to offer her now than he'd had back when they'd been engaged. Less of the things she deserved, such as security, money and a shot at a normal life.

ALEX WAS ADJUSTING THE VOLUME on the boom box that she used for her weekly music class when she heard her mother returning with the nesting drum set she'd asked Yetta to bring over. She'd decided to tie in this week's lesson with the "Little Drummer Boy" song.

She pressed the pause button and turned around.

"Thanks..." she said, her voice trailing off when she realized her mother wasn't alone. Like an un-uniformed porter, Mark was laden with bongos and tambourines, and tucked under each arm were the miniature congas the kids adored.

"Oh, goodness, you didn't need to bring the entire rhythm section," she said, hurrying to help. "But the children will thank you for it. They all love to pound on drums, and sharing isn't a concept most three-year-olds readily embrace."

Mark handed her a couple of the smaller drums. "Where do you want these? I bumped into your mom outside and she asked for a hand."

"I knew the children would enjoy each having an instrument," Yetta said. "Mark is very strong. We managed this in one trip."

Alex spread the drums about in front of the yellow outline of the sun on the group rug. Her day-care students were resting in the smaller common room, and her preschool students were outside with Rita and the aides. They'd be back any minute, full of energy.

"Thanks, Mom. I really need to buy another storage shed."

Her mother added the two small drums she was carrying to the circle. "I thought you were going to convert the small bedroom into a storeroom."

Alex's house had four bedrooms. The one her mother was referring to served as an office and a guest room, but eventually, Alex planned to turn it into a nursery. "Um, yeah, but I still have a few overnighters once in a while."

She looked at Mark and added, "Children. Children whose parents for some reason can't pick them up. Doesn't happen often, but the extra bed comes in handy."

She blushed when she realized her hasty explanation sounded defensive. Brushing a few stray cookie crumbs off her jeans, she glanced at the big clock on the wall and said, "You're here awfully early. Did something happen?"

"Um, yeah. I've been relieved of duty. Protocol. Best for all concerned, they told me. But, luckily for me, the suspension is with pay. So, since I don't have to go out and get a job flipping burgers to pay the rent, I'm available to help here. If you want me."

Alex swallowed. Want him? What woman in her right mind wouldn't want a man like Mark? But none of those women had had her heart broken by him. Could Alex handle working side by side with him? Indulging in one night of secret sexual fantasies was one thing, but working together was something wholly different.

She looked at her mother, who was watching them both. "Why don't you give it a try and see how it goes?" Yetta suggested. "Mark may change his mind about helping after he's sat through one music class."

Alex glanced down at the circle of drums and stifled a smile. Her mother was right. Music day. Trial by fire…

Chapter Nine

The pounding and crashing disharmony erupted like small, individual explosions behind his eyes. A dozen or more three- and four-year-olds with drums. What was Alex thinking?

And, more importantly, where were her earplugs?

She held up her hand and said something that got swallowed up by the noise, then, to his surprise, the drumbeats lessened. Heads turned to look at her—a smiling pillar in jeans and a purple Dancing Hippo T-shirt.

"Remember. We start off every music class by listening," she said, enunciating the last word loudly and succinctly.

The last drummer—a red-haired boy with a wild look in his eyes—put his hands in his lap, with assistance from a helper, who looked enough like the child to be his mother. "Sorry," the woman murmured.

"Very good. You're all using your ears." Alex tucked her wavy black hair back and pushed on her ears so they appeared to wiggle. "Me, too."

The children giggled and followed suit.

"Where's Uncle Claude?" the redhead asked. "He has jumbo ears. I miss him."

Alex made her bottom lip curl sadly. "Me, too, William.

Maybe if everyone writes him a letter, we can send it to my cousin's ranch where Uncle is visiting and he'll come back to see us."

Mark vaguely remembered Claude Radonovic as a jovial fellow with a big laugh. He didn't recall the size of his ears. Zeke had mentioned that Claude had been caught in the undercover sting that Grace's future husband had orchestrated. Apparently, he'd provided information to the D.A. in exchange for no jail time. Instead, he'd been required to remain on his son's ranch.

Changing the topic, Alex leaned forward as if to pick up her instrument—a lilac-colored tambourine adorned with multicolored silk ribbons. He could picture her dancing in costume to the passionate beat of the flamenco. God, he'd loved watching her dance.

"Wait," she said, her hands hovering over the drum. "We are going to take turns as we learn a new song. I'll sing it first, then we'll do it together. You only touch the drum when you hear me say 'bar-rump-a-bum-bum.' Okay?"

Nearly every head nodded.

She cleared her throat and sang in a clear, crisp alto the words to a Christmas song that Mark had heard a thousand times, but never really listened to. "Come, they told me…"

Little hands flew with joy, but no rhythm.

Alex lifted her hands. The discord stopped.

He braced himself for the next cacophony, but each drum session seemed a little more musical. By the last verse, the children seemed to have caught on and were actually trying to copy Alex.

"Yeah," she cried, cheering joyfully. "You were marvelous. Next time, we'll sound like a real band."

She pulled what looked like a stopwatch from her

pocket and said, "Okay. Two minutes of freestyle then we put away the drums. One, two, three…go."

She scrambled to her feet and backed up, covering her ears. The aides did the same, and Mark quickly followed suit. He walked to where Alex was standing. "Nice," he mouthed.

"Thank you," she returned.

He decided there was something to be said for lip-reading—especially lips as pretty and voluptuous as Alex's. Their gazes met for just a moment. She turned away. Had she read his mind? She'd always been good at that. Too good, at times.

After the two minutes of mind-numbing noise had passed, she blew a whistle. The drumming ceased—even the redhead kid stopped, thanks to his resourceful mother who snatched up the drum and walked away. The look on her face said she was trying to be a good sport, but the whole thing might be more than she could take. He knew the feeling.

While Alex and her helpers got the children organized and washed up for a snack, Mark repackaged the drums. The mother who was volunteering stayed with him. "You're new here," she said. "Which of these little darlings is yours?"

"My son attends the after-school session. I was curious about the preschool, and Miss Alex said I could drop in to check things out."

"Oh, you'll be bringing your son's younger sibling, I take it. William wants a baby sister, but some days I'm convinced one is my limit. How many do you and your wife have?"

"My ex-wife—Braden's mother—isn't in the picture. He's an only child."

She nodded with a sort of resigned manner. "Oh. We see that a lot. More and more single fathers with full custody."

She started pointing out which children came from broken homes. Mark decided he didn't like this woman, who hadn't even told him her name.

Alex suddenly appeared and lightly touched the woman's arm. "Roberta, you're so good at getting the children settled in their chairs, would you mind…? Thanks, you're a gem."

"Of course, Alex, I'd be happy to," the woman— Roberta—said before marching off to do her duty.

A gem?

Alex looked at him, a wry grin on her lips, as if she'd heard his silent question. "Volunteers are an important part of our program. Good for the parents to be involved and good for the children. Plus, the extra help allows me to keep my prices down, which is particularly important to single parents."

"I understand that, but do you ever think the moms are more work than the kids?" he asked, leaning in to keep the comment just between them.

Her low chuckle crept into his chest and traveled lower. "Occasionally," she admitted. "But sometimes it's a toss-up."

She nodded slightly, and Mark looked past her to the three round tables with the small, primary-colored chairs. Roberta and her son seemed to be conducting a silent but intense war of wills. The mother won, but not without picking up her son and depositing him in the chair.

Mark smiled and was about to comment when Alex dashed off. A little girl, the last in line at the sink, lost her balance and tumbled to the floor. Heedless of the puddles that had accumulated around the base of the basin, Alex dropped to her bottom and pulled the crying child into her lap.

White-blond curls melded with Alex's shorter black ones as she commiserated with the little girl. Mark's heart returned to a normal beat as soon as he realized there wasn't any real injury, but a tightness in his chest remained. The feeling was one he didn't recognize at first, then it hit him. Love. He was back in love with Alex. Correction. He was *still* in love with Alex.

ALEX HAD A HEADACHE. A stress headache, she decided. She could handle music class with fourteen overly ambitious, untrained drummers. She could handle bumps and bruises and hypochondriac mothers who thought every sore limb needed an X-ray. But she couldn't handle having Mark around full-time.

He was too large. Too dynamic. Too charming. By nap time, Alex swore every one of her aides—even Rita, who would turn sixty-eight next month—was in love with him.

Without noticeable effort, he'd even won over Roberta Moorehouse, despite the fact that Alex was certain Mark thought the woman was a gossipy twit.

"Headache?" a voice asked.

Alex, who had been staring at her computer screen trying to decide whether or not to switch to a different brand of finger paint, looked up. "Oh, hi, Mom. I thought you went home."

"I did, but Katherine called to ask if I'd pick up Maya after school, and I thought I'd come over early so I could meet Mark's son. Is he here?"

Alex's heart jumped in panic—for a second. Then she remembered. "Mark and Maya went to meet him. They'll be back any second."

The brief rush of adrenaline magnified her headache, but she did her best to pretend she was fine.

"Alexandra, even the strongest amongst us resort to aspirin on occasion. A little painkiller won't inhibit your ability to conceive."

Alex felt her mouth drop open. The worst part of being Romani was the inability to keep anything private. From anybody. "How did you—?" She closed her eyes and shook her head. Why ask?

"Darling girl, you're my firstborn. I knew this day was coming. With your sisters' situations and all the talk in women's magazines about biological clocks and whatnot, I'd expected it before now."

"Really? You don't think I'm being foolish? Or selfish? Depriving a child of a two-parent family?"

Her mother smiled indulgently. "You are the least selfish person I know. I am, of course, worried about what this will mean to your health. A headache is one thing, but I remember all too well how debilitating the pain was before your operation. And I also remember the doctors telling you there was no guarantee the growths wouldn't come back if you stopped taking the birth-control pills."

"I know, Mom. But you always encouraged us to face the challenges in our lives head-on. The first time I had stage fright you told me, 'You can either get out on that stage and dance, or you can look back someday and wish you had.'"

Yetta bent down and put her hand over Alex's. "Speaking of dance, Grace has invited a band to play at the charity Christmas dinner at Romantique. She wants the Sisters of the Silver Dollar to perform."

Alex groaned. As children, she and her sisters had danced for their father and he would toss coins at their feet.

Big, shiny silver dollars that had been used in slot machines at that time. Eventually, the girls had developed several routines and danced at family functions. They'd kept the name: the Sisters of the Silver Dollar.

"That's big of her. I was planning on doing nothing for two full weeks."

Yetta chuckled and patted Alex's hand. "Now, now, your sister has her own travails. She puts on a good show, but she's very lonely. And she misses the restaurant. If it weren't for this wedding she's planning, I'm sure she and Nikolai would be miserable."

Alex nodded. "That's true. When Grace is miserable, everybody is miserable."

"That's why I've decided to fly to Detroit to spend a few days with her."

Alex pushed back from her desk in shock. "That's sudden."

"Jurek called and suggested it. He claims to have frequent flier miles to use up and bought me the ticket. I think he's lonely, too, although he won't admit it."

Jurek was Yetta's cousin several times removed. He was also Nikolai's birth father, although the two had only recently been reunited. Yetta and Jurek had grown quite close during the Charles Harmon fiasco, with Jurek moving next door into Claude's empty house so Yetta could help him recover his strength after some sort of surgery.

Jurek's quick trip to Michigan to see Nick and Grace had been extended when Nick's adoptive parents, who had recently retired, had asked him to house-sit while they went traveling.

"Wow. Well, that's great. Grace will be over the moon."

"I know she was just here, but we never really had a chance

to talk. We might even find a wedding dress. And since you have Mark here to help, you should be just fine, right?"

Mark. The man she'd pretty well decided to ask not to come back, except to drop off and pick up his son.

Yetta leaned closer and said in a low voice, "Alexandra, be careful not to let the past obscure your view of the present. He's not the man he used to be, any more than you're the same girl you were eight years ago."

And, as if her mother had conjured him up, Mark walked through the door, preceded by two children, who were holding hands. Alex couldn't prevent the smile that seemed to magically ease her headache. A smile that matched the happy look on Braden's face. A first. A joyful first.

"Is Rob picking up Maya after work?" she asked on impulse.

Yetta shook her head. "He's in the Bay Area on business. Katherine will be by after the restaurant closes."

"Then, let's go out for dinner. You, me, Mark and the kids. Somewhere fun."

Mark, who'd just returned from the coatroom, seconded her suggestion. "Good idea. Braden likes the buffet at the Palace Station."

"I believe I have some coupons," Yetta said. "I'll be right back. You two can work out the details."

Something about the way her mother phrased her comment made Alex think that Yetta didn't intend to join them, but that was okay, too. Mark needed cheering up, and Alex wasn't the kind of person who lied to herself. She enjoyed his company—even if working with him on a regular basis might mean stocking up on aspirin.

Chapter Ten

"Daddy Rob is a lawyer. My other daddy lives in Reno. That's a long way from here, but we're going to drive there after Auntie Grace's wedding. Mommy says we can't go before then because Grace would track her down with a knife." She smiled. "Not really. But that's what Mommy said."

Mark was mesmerized by the articulate cherub sitting across from him at the Palace Station. The dining hall was massive and you practically needed a map to find the various food selections, but feeding Braden and Maya had been easy: pizza, burgers, spaghetti and Jell-O.

Since Yetta had bowed out at the last minute, Alex had insisted that Mark fill his own plate while she waited at the table with the kids. His choices included shrimp scampi, rare prime rib, filet mignon wrapped in bacon, garlic mashed potatoes and several types of vegetables, along with a separate plate loaded with salads. Alex had yet to return from her culinary quest.

"I haven't seen your mother or Grace in quite a while, but…" he said, after chewing and swallowing a bite of steak. "I can't picture either one with a knife."

"How come?" Maya asked, pulling free a piece of pep-peroni, which she delicately nibbled on.

"Because they're not the violent type."

"I mean how come you haven't seen them for a long time?"

Oh. He looked at Braden who had his hands wrapped around a burger. "I was busy with my family and my job."

"Did you stop being friends with Aunt Alex?"

"You could say that."

"How come?"

Damn, this girl was going to be a reporter when she grew up. "I...think we should talk about you. What's Santa bringing you for Christmas?"

She abruptly dropped her chin and didn't say anything for a full minute. When she looked up, her big brown eyes were filled with tears that looked ready to spill over the rims. Mark had no idea what he'd said to make her cry. "Maya, what's wrong?"

"William Moorehouse said Santa isn't real. He said mom-mies and daddies put presents under the tree and say they're from Santa, but they...they're..." Her voice turned thin and thready. "N-not." The last word came out with a hiccup.

Mark looked at Braden, whose bottom lip was begin-ning to quiver. *Alex...help.*

As if she'd heard his silent plea, Alex strolled up to their table and set down her heaping plate, but before she could sit, Maya burst into tears. Braden followed suit, less noisily, but salty drops started falling onto his pasta.

"Maya, love, what's wrong? Bray? Yikes. Is the food that bad?" She dashed around the table so she was si-tuated between them and placed one arm around each child. "Kiddos, please. Tell me what's going on?" They both collapsed against her shoulders. Only then did she look at Mark.

He squeezed the bridge of his nose. "A certain little Scrooge at school told Maya there wasn't a Santa Claus."

"Oh. *Oh.* I bet I know who. But that doesn't matter. What matters is he was wrong." Maya picked up her head. "I know there's a Santa. I've met him."

Braden looked at Maya, his expression as skeptical as hers. Maya put their question into words. "Not the store Santa. The *real* Santa who lives at the North Pole."

Alex nodded. "Yep. That one. When I was about Braden's age I caught him putting presents under our tree and we had a nice long talk." She stood up quickly to avoid a server hurrying past with a pitcher of water. "I'll tell you the story while you finish eating. Did you see the dessert bar? Ohmygosh, there's a zillion things to try."

Braden picked up his fork. Maya let out a weighty sigh and did the same. Alex looked at Mark as she pulled up her chair and folded her napkin in her lap. He could see the sparkle in her eyes and wondered just how she was going to pull this potential tragedy out of the fire.

"Do you mind if I talk and eat at the same time?" she asked, taking a bite of sushi that she'd mixed with wasabi and soy sauce. Her eyes went wide as she chewed, but after a minute she said, "Umm. Good. Okay, where was I? The night I met Santa…"

Mark ate, but he really didn't taste anything after that point. He was too wrapped up in her story, which he realized was a clever mix of fact and fantasy. She made it sound so real he could almost picture her sneaking up on the man in red, who had been distributing packages wrapped in the same paper her mother had used.

"What did he say?" Maya asked.

"He took me on his knee—just like the store Santa does, and said, 'Alexandra—' he knew my name '—your parents and I work together. You write me a letter with what you want and I make sure they have the means to get things. But only *we* know about your *secret* wish.'"

Maya and Braden both sat forward. "What was it?"

"A pogo stick." Blushing, she hastily looked at Mark then explained, "I wanted one so badly, but I didn't tell anybody because was afraid I'd look funny bouncing around. I was kinda chubby back then, and I thought everybody would make fun of me."

Aw... Mark thought, his heart breaking on her behalf.

Maya looked at Braden a moment then said, "Braden wants to know if he brought you one."

"Next time, let him ask," Alex gently reprimanded. "But the answer is yes. The next morning after we were all done opening presents, my dad said, 'Wait. What's this? An un- wrapped box, but there's a name on it. To Alex, from Santa.'"

Maya clapped. "A pogo stick. And you bounced around on it."

"You're right. I did. And my cousins laughed. One of them said, 'Ha. Ha. That's not something you see every day—a hippo on a stick.'"

Braden and Maya exchanged some kind of silent com- munication then both dug into their food. As Alex finished off the last of her Creole shrimp, she gave Mark a very self- satisfied look. He silently applauded her. She'd neatly put the question of Santa's identity aside for another year, plus she'd given the children back a little magic of the holiday. If he hadn't loved her before, this evening would have sealed his fate.

Later, as they followed Braden and Maya through the dessert queue, Mark said, "Good save back there. Didn't really happen though, right?"

She gave him a shocked look. "Of course it did. Many, many years later, I found out that I'd accidentally bumped into Uncle Claude that night. It had been his turn to play Santa for several Rom families, and he'd been so upset by my tearful admission that he came back later with the pogo stick he'd bought for Gregor. He was afraid I'd figure out the truth if he left it wrapped in the paper my aunt was using that year, so he unwrapped it and scribbled my name on the box."

Mark started laughing, but quickly sobered when the children gave him a suspicious look. "Poor Greg. Did he ever find out?"

Alex, with a twinkle in her eyes, shook her head. "Never. And don't you tell him. He's been through enough disappointment in his life lately."

Over crème brûlée, chocolate torte and apple pie, he asked her to explain her comment about her cousin. The children were standing a few feet away taking turns darting back and forth under a rope partition. Their bowls of mostly melted ice cream that had been laden with M&M's looked like confetti soup.

"MaryAnn, Greg's wife, had a nervous breakdown about six months ago. She'd been depressed after her father died, and then her mother sold everything and moved to Hawaii. Not long after that, Gregor lost his job and got picked up for some stupid infraction. She was working for Charles Harmon at the time and saw a way to make some money by blackmailing him."

Mark had heard that part of the story from Zeke. "Not a good idea. He's a very bad man."

"We all found out how bad, but poor MaryAnn was certain her family would be better off without her. She went to our houseboat to end it all, but Nick—going on a hunch Grace had—got there in time." She sighed. "You know Grace—has to be involved in everybody's business." She said it in a way that told him how much she loved her sister.

"Unfortunately, MaryAnn wound up shooting Grace—accidentally, of course. Rob, my new brother-in-law, argued in her defense and made a deal with the prosecutor, so MaryAnn got the help she needed instead of going to jail."

"How is she now? Not living at home, I gather."

"Not yet, but Gregor is hopeful she'll be back by Christmas."

Tracey had admitted herself into a treatment center a few months before she'd died. Mark had hoped and prayed the treatment would get her off drugs. For a short time, he'd actually believed her when she'd said she was clean. But then he'd got the call from Tracey's neighbor telling him Odessa had shown up claiming Tracey was dead.

"Luca seems like a great kid. I hope things work out."

He spotted a waiter giving the children an unhappy look, so he wiped his lips with his napkin and said, "Should we go? The natives are getting restless."

Alex nodded. "Aye, Captain, juvenile meltdown quickly approaching Mach speed. We're gonna lose 'em," she said with a *Star Trek* impersonation.

Mark just shook his head.

As they headed to the door, the children holding hands between them, Alex said, "Seriously, Mark, thanks for this. I'd planned to pay, you know."

He shook his head. "My pleasure. I mean that. Evenings

tend to get bit long with a couple of bachelors hanging out."

Especially when one half of the odd couple doesn't talk.

She smiled as if hearing his unspoken qualifier and softly said, "He will."

Her conviction made him want to believe—in Braden and in Santa. He'd been several years younger than Maya when he'd learned the truth about Christmas. No matter how good you tried to be, you could never be good enough.

Christmas and New Year's had never been his favorite time of year. Depressing memories crowded out the few good ones he'd made with Alex. The night he and Tracey had got together was after a drinking binge of comparing worst-holiday stories. Not that that excused what he'd done, but the memory gave him one more reason to hate the holidays.

"Good thing we brought two cars," Alex said, drawing him back to the present. "I see two kids who are going to be asleep by the time we leave the parking lot."

He agreed and bent down to pick up Maya when the child stumbled and nearly fell as they approached the exit. "Are you taking her home or back to Yetta's house?"

"Home. She'll sleep better in her own bed. I'll just curl up on Kate's couch and read until her mother gets there."

The night wind held a bite, and they didn't speak again until they reached their cars. Mark had driven his sedan instead of the pickup truck. The car had been Tracey's. Odessa still claimed she should have inherited it, but since Mark had been the one to pay for it and since his name was still on the registration, he'd kept it.

He helped Maya into Alex's car then made sure Braden's seat belt was fastened. He and Alex were standing between the two cars, shivering. He wasn't sure what to say.

"I'll see you tomorrow, okay?"

She opened her mouth as if to say something, but apparently changed her mind and nodded. "Yeah. Tomorrow."

ALEX HAD BEEN RIGHT about one thing—Maya was asleep before they were a mile down the road. This meant Alex had to make the long drive to the Lakes, a high-end development northeast of Henderson, in silence. With only her thoughts to occupy her.

Thoughts like… *What the heck is wrong with me?* Socializing with a single father whose child went to her school was bad enough, but when that father was the man who'd broken her heart, the situation was untenable. She probably needed her head examined.

"Maybe I should go visit MaryAnn and see if her shrink could spare a minute or two for me," she mumbled under her breath.

Not that she hadn't had a wonderful time tonight. Mark had managed to keep the conversation going without excluding the kids. She hadn't met a lot of men who bothered to do that. When children were around, they usually talked down to them or ignored them.

How had he learned to be such a good parent when he'd had such a poor role model? she wondered.

The question was still on her mind three hours later when Kate arrived home. "You're early. Quiet night at Romantique?" she asked, following the sounds coming from the kitchen.

Kate looked up around the door of the fridge. "Hi. Want some juice?"

Alex shook her head. "No, thanks, but Liz would be proud seeing you pick OJ over soda."

"Yeah, I got tired of her nagging," Kate said, pouring the pulpy liquid into a glass. "Turns out my husband is something of a health nut, too, but he's from California so what can you expect?"

She took a long drink then let out a sigh. "Actually, we were packed on the main floor and had two parties in the private rooms. This is the first year I've had businesses book their staff parties mid-week." She polished off the juice then said, "Fortunately, we've added a couple of people to the crew. Our new hostess is nowhere near as outgoing and charming as Grace, but she kept things moving pretty well."

"Grace really misses her old job."

Kate nodded. "I know. It was just like old times when she filled in last weekend. I was a little leery about suggesting the idea to Jo. I was afraid she might feel weird since Grace used to be Jo's employer. But my mother-in-law is amazing. Totally fine with it. We had a blast."

"That's good."

Kate nodded, her mop of curls bouncing. Even from across the room, Alex could smell the scents of the kitchen that clung to her sister's checkered pants and white chef's shirt.

"Maya's in bed."

"Thanks. You didn't have to bring her home, but I appreciate it. A lot. I hate coming in to a dark house when Rob is gone. Funny how quickly you get fixed in a routine."

Alex couldn't prevent a little stab of envy. Her house would be black and cold when she got home. *If not for Tracey*— She pushed the thought away, but some telling hint must have shown on her face because Kate said, "Let's sit at the breakfast nook. I want to hear about tonight and, more importantly, what's going on with you and Mark.

When Mom called to get permission for you to take Maya to dinner, I nearly dropped a pan of lasagna."

"It was a spur-of-the-moment decision. Mom was supposed to join us but suddenly remembered a date with Zeke."

Kate looked thoughtful. "Sounds as if she's playing matchmaker, but that seems unlikely given what happened between you two. You're not…um, dating him, are you?"

"Two kids don't make for a terribly romantic meal," Alex said, sidestepping the question.

Kate's chuckle got lost in a yawn. "Very true."

Neither spoke for a minute or two, then Kate said, "Alex, you know I'm not the prying kind, but if you ever want to talk about what's going on in your life, I'd be happy to listen. We've both had our share of heartbreak, and I'm living proof that good things happen if you hang in there."

Alex smiled. She and Kate had never been close, but she liked her second-to-youngest sister—a lot. "For a minute there I thought you were going to say you were living proof that prophecies come true."

"There were times when I was convinced that Mom had copied mine off a fortune cookie, but then Rob and Ian both showed up in my life and I realized I really did have to fix the past before I could move forward." She sighed as if glad to have all of that controversy behind her, then asked, "What's yours again? I swear my brain is mushy from inhaling too much oregano."

Alex laughed and stood up. "You're just tired. Go to bed. We'll talk later. I'm going home. I need to get some sleep, too. Nothing like two dozen kids wired on holiday hype to wear you down in a hurry."

She gave her sister a hug then left. She'd planned to talk

about Mark—get Kate's take on the subject, but at the last minute she'd changed her mind. Tempting though it was to think that maybe she and Mark had a chance at a do-over, the hard reality was too much had changed in their lives. She had a plan and she needed to stick to it. If she survived the holidays—and more importantly, if she made it through her period without pain—she would set her plan in motion. She didn't need Mark—or any man—in her life to do that.

Chapter Eleven

"I'm curious about something, Mark. Why'd you change jobs? I thought you liked being a cop."

Nearly a week had passed since their dinner out with the kids. Mark had continued to show up at the Hippo each afternoon a couple of hours before Braden arrived. At the moment, he was assembling cardboard boxes that the children would decorate and use for the plaster of Paris handprint wall-hanging that they'd spent three art classes making and painting.

"Parts of the job were great, but dealing with the public can get old. A fire doesn't talk back," he quipped, looking up from the lid he'd just finished folding. He dropped it on the box he'd completed moments earlier then picked up another flat piece of cardboard. "Tracey was afraid she'd get passed over for advancement if we were in the same department. So, I took the test, passed it without a problem and made the switch."

His broad shoulders lifted and fell in a careless shrug. "Turned out to be the right move."

Alex was at her desk sealing past-due invoices in envelopes that she would personally hand to the parents after school. The process made her feel like a grinch, but late charges were a part of doing business—even at the holidays. "I'm glad to hear that. I was afraid my dad might have influenced your decision. He gave you a lot of grief about being in Metro."

Mark chuckled. "That he did. Good ol' Ernst…never met a cop he didn't hate."

"He wasn't *quite* that bad, and in your case, part of his attitude came from the fact that you wanted to marry his daughter."

He smiled at her in a way that made her wish she could turn back the hands of the clock. Ernst would have liked the man Mark had become—she was sure of it.

"Actually, *my* old man was the reason I chose law enforcement in the first place. I wanted to prove to him that I could make something of my life, and being a cop seemed like the furthest opposite of his life as possible."

"Yeah, I remember you being pretty gung ho when we were dating."

"Gung ho? That's an understatement. I was intensely focused on my career at the time."

"I didn't mean it as a criticism."

"I know. You're too polite. But even if Tracey hadn't pushed me to change jobs, I would have been looking for something different after Braden was born. I discovered that I liked being a dad and the fire department offered better hours."

"Ah, good point. Was it tough to make the transition?"

"My friends in the force thought I was nuts, but Zeke was in my corner. I think he pulled a few strings to get me into the arson unit."

"It occurred to me that you might not be a suspect if you were still working at Metro."

He shook his head. "Wouldn't have changed anything. The minute my name came up, the detectives on the case had to follow through. I wouldn't have done anything differently if it was my case. Unfortunately, I don't have an alibi for that night. After my shift was over, I went home, ate dinner, watched some TV and went to bed. Like usual. I called Tracey's to talk to Braden, but there wasn't any answer. I figured Tracey was screening her calls and avoiding me because of something that had happened earlier in the week."

"What happened?"

He frowned. "A friend who works in the Clark County High Density Drug Trafficking Area told me Tracey's name had shown up during surveillance of a particularly notorious part of town. Lots of drug traffic. No arrests were made, but photos were taken, and Tracey was easy to spot since she used to be a cop."

"What did she say when you confronted her?"

"The usual. That she'd been there looking for a friend who was having a hard time staying clean. She was adamant that she hadn't done drugs in two months." He looked down. "In hindsight it sounds naive on my part, but I believed her. She actually seemed to be getting her act together."

Neither spoke for a minute, then Mark said, "Meth is bad stuff. Fairly easy to make, although volatile as hell. A lot of the street meth in this area comes from super labs in Mexico, but we see our share of *methmaticians* here, too."

Alex started to ask about the friend Tracey had claimed to be looking for when Mark's cell phone rang. He looked at the number on the display and groaned. "Odessa. The woman is totally whacked. She thinks if I go to jail she'll get custody of Braden, but I'll be damned if I let that happen. She ruined one kid and she's never going to get her hands on my son."

Alex had never heard him speak as harshly, not even when he talked about his father.

Mark pocketed the phone then stood up. "Where do you want these? I'd better get out to the bus. I wouldn't put it past Odessa to abduct Braden if she saw her chance."

"Does she know that he's going to school here?"

Mark shook his head. "I don't think so, but the woman is surprisingly resourceful for a habitual drug user. She found out about my suspension almost before I did." His expression turned dark. "Tracey still had a few friends on the force when she died. I have a feeling someone is feeding Odessa information."

Alex made a mental note to remind her staff that Braden was never to be released to anyone but his father. This Odessa woman sounded like someone Alex didn't want to meet.

She finished sealing the envelopes and pushed back her chair to stand up. A pain jabbed her in the left side midway between her pelvis and ribs, making her cry out softly. She was anticipating the arrival of her first regular period since stopping the pill with mixed emotions. Getting back onto a normal cycle would be good—as long as the horrific pain she remembered from before didn't return, too.

"Rita? Will you keep an eye on things a minute? I need something from my room."

Her second-in-charge nodded and returned her attention to helping the five children at her table work on their number skills.

Alex pressed her fingers beneath the waistband of her jeans. No swelling that she could detect, but the area was tender. *Just typical PMS,* she told herself.

She took a couple of over-the-counter painkillers and returned to the classroom. Even before she stepped from the hallway to the main room, she could tell something had changed. The energy in the room fairly crackled.

Hurrying, she looked around. Rita and her group of students were at the front window looking out, along with both of her other aides. "What's happening?"

"Two police cars just pulled up," Rita said.

Alex didn't bother with the window. She raced to the door, grabbing her wool sweater from the back of her desk chair. Before she'd taken two steps toward the gate, a third car pulled into the cul-de-sac. Zeke.

She knew without a doubt this had to do with Mark. He should have been back from the bus stop by now, she thought, hurrying across the wet grass to the far corner of the yard where she could see the street in both directions. A block away, a large orange bus was lumbering off.

The bigger bus was Luca's. Lately, Mark had taken to waiting for the older boy to arrive from school, hoping Braden and Luca would become better acquainted. Had Mark seen the cops?

She watched the three figures turn and start toward the school. Mark was too far away for her to see his expression, but she could tell by the way his shoulders were set that he was bracing himself for something bad.

She hurried back to the gate and stepped out. "Zeke," she called. "What's going on?"

The silver-haired detective joined her. "The informant who gave us Mark's name was found dead this morning. Gunshot."

"That's too bad, but surely you don't think Mark did it?"

Zeke's face was unreadable, but Alex could tell that he

was upset. "We have to bring him in for questioning. Procedure. If his alibi checks out, he'll be out in a couple of hours."

"You're going to take him away in a police car?" she cried. "In front of his son? No way. That isn't right. Zeke, please, I'm begging you. Let Mark come inside and get Braden settled, then he can come back here and leave with you."

Zeke's gaze was on the man walking between two little boys. Mark appeared at ease, although Alex could tell he wasn't.

"This dog-and-pony show wasn't my idea," Zeke said, his voice harsh. "I'll keep them off his tail for ten minutes."

Impulsively, Alex rose up on her toes to kiss his leathery cheek. "Thanks." Then, she dashed to the corner to intercept Mark and the boys.

"Hi, guys. Lots of excitement today. We have to hurry and get inside, then Mark is going to come back and go with the police to help them."

"Help them do what?" Luca asked.

"Solve a crime. Zeke couldn't tell me all the details, but Mark is the only one who can help them find the bad guy."

Mark hesitated, as if not sure whether to accompany her inside or not. She grabbed his arm and plastered herself to his side as she took Braden's hand. "This is a really important job. I know you'll have a wild story to tell us when you get back, but we need to chat a minute before you leave. Okay?"

He was close enough for her see the fine greenish gold tint to his irises. Such pretty eyes for a man, she'd always thought. Now, those eyes were narrowed with concern. "Sure," he said, not even looking toward the police cars.

Alex did, though. Zeke was engaged in an animated discussion with two uniformed policemen and one female officer. The woman seemed visibly upset.

"That was Tracey's best friend when she was on the force. Can't remember her name," Mark said, as he and Alex waited for Braden and Luca to walk into the building ahead of them.

"You're not surprised she put on a big show to arrest you?" she asked.

He nodded. "Zeke called me on my cell as I was waiting for the bus. He wasn't sure he'd get here in time to help." His lips quivered a second then turned up. "I should have told him not to bother since you had raced to my rescue."

She wasn't sure whether to laugh or cry. "What happens now? Are they arresting you?"

"I don't know what's going to happen." He closed the door and turned to look her in the eyes. "Will you keep Braden if this runs long? I hate to ask, but I really don't have a choice. I'm sorry. I know you don't feel too hot today."

His observation surprised her. She thought she'd hidden her symptoms well, but apparently not that well. "I'm fine. A little PMS. Braden can stay as long as it takes. I have a whole drawer of extra kids' clothes that I've accumulated over the years. Not to worry."

He nodded. "Thanks. That means a lot to me. Now, I'd better get inside and make up something to tell him."

"Tell him the truth—well, as close to the truth as you can. I think he's comfortable enough with me that he won't feel abandoned."

He put his hand on the small of her back and leaned around her to open the door. His lips brushed past her ear and he added, "You're a lifesaver, Alex. Thank you."

Then he kissed her.

Just a peck. Hopefully hidden from the cops on the

street. But a sweet taste of the past—of what they'd almost had. And couldn't have again, she reminded herself as she hurried inside.

Fortunately, she had her hands full calming the children and getting their focus off the flashing lights on the street.

"Everybody, where are your ears?" she asked, putting both hands to either side of her head. "What do we do with our ears?"

"Listen," the high-pitched chorus cried.

"Good. Then come to the circle and sit down, and while we talk about the police officers who are helpers in our lives, Miss Rita will get our snack ready. Luca, Maya, will you join us, please? Braden can come when he's done talking with his daddy."

Maya, who had been part of the group at the window until her friend walked inside, didn't appear anxious to leave Braden's side. "But Auntie Alex—"

"Can you come by yourself or do you need my help?"

With a dramatic sigh, the little girl trudged across the room and sat down—well away from Alex. Luca, who usually stayed at the "big kid" table, sat down beside her.

"Thank you. Now, who can tell me what kinds of officers were outside just now?"

"I know. I know," William shouted. "Police."

Mark heard the word reverberate through the connected rooms, but his attention was focused on his son. How did he tell Braden that he might be arrested?

He pulled up one of the spare chairs and sat down, his knees practically touching his chest. "Bray, I have to go with Zeke. You remember him, don't you? He's a police officer. Like Mommy used to be."

Braden had hung up his coat and turned to face Mark.

Even though no question came from his son's lips, Mark could hear the big "Why?"

"I don't know exactly what's going to happen, son. I might be there a couple of hours, maybe even overnight. But Alex said you could stay with her for however long this takes. Are you okay with that? You like her. You're safe here. Everything will be okay. I promise."

Mark held out his arms. "Hug goodbye?"

Braden ran to him. His thin arms squeezed Mark tightly. Mark was blinking back tears when he looked up and spotted Zeke in the doorway of the cloakroom. He kissed his son then turned him around and pointed him toward the rug with the sunshine circle. "Be good for Alex. I love you, Braden."

Chapter Twelve

"Hey, cuz, Luca told me about the excitement around here this afternoon. You and the kid okay over there?"

Alex smiled at the phone. "We're fine, Gregor. Thanks for asking. Braden just had a bath and is getting his pajamas on. A hand-me-down pair from Luca, I think. Something with *Star Wars* figures on it."

"Sounds like Luca's. He was pretty upset that the cops took Braden's dad away. What was that all about?"

"They took him for questioning. I don't know the details, and I haven't heard anything since they left."

"Does this have to do with the kid's mom's death?"

"I think so."

Her cousin let out a soft groan. "Man, and I thought my life was screwed up. At least my wife is getting better." He paused then added, "Did I tell you the doctor said MaryAnn could come home for the holidays? Two full weeks. And if she does okay, she'll be able to stay for good."

Alex finished drying the skillet she'd used for their hamburgers. She'd been afraid Braden would be too upset to eat, but the child had finished off every bite of his sandwich and a good-size mound of green beans. Even Maya turned her nose up at vegetables.

"That's wonderful news, Gregor. When do you pick her up?"

"Saturday. I was going to throw a party, but your mother said we should play it low-key to let MaryAnn settle back. Smart woman, your mother."

"I agree. Besides, MaryAnn will see everybody at Christmas, right? That's only thirteen days away."

"Don't remind me. I haven't bought any presents. I wanted to, but then I thought maybe that's something MaryAnn and I should do together. But you know how stressful shopping is. The people, the noise…the money. It's gonna be a little skimpy under our tree unless Santa hits the lotto."

Unless Santa hits the lotto? Oh, no, does that mean Greg is gambling again? As if in answer to her unasked question, he said, "I meant the North Pole Santa, not me. I haven't laid a wager since MaryAnn went to Montevista."

Alex believed him. Although her cousin had been a carefree goof-off as a kid and downright lazy and immature as an adult, he'd changed after nearly losing MaryAnn. That near-miss had made him grow up.

"I'm really glad to hear that, Greg. MaryAnn is going to be so proud of you." Before she could add that the whole family was proud of him, Braden walked in. Damp blond hair sticking up in all directions. His plastic-soled sleepers made a scratching sound against the tile floor. He looked at her and smiled, and Alex's voice left her.

Coughing into her hand, she said, "My houseguest is here. Gotta go. Thanks for checking on us."

"No problem. Call if you hear from Mark or you need anything. Braden could come over here, if you have to go pick him up or anything."

"Sweet of you to offer, but I think we'll be fine. Night."

She hung up the phone then walked to where Braden was standing, looking a little lost. "Nice jammies. They fit perfectly. They were Luca's, you know."

Braden looked down and pointed to the image of a young boy with blond hair. Alex had seen all the *Star Wars* movies, but wasn't a huge fan of the most recent trilogy, so she couldn't tell him the character's name, if that was what he was asking. "I don't know who that is. He looks a little bit like you, though, doesn't he?"

Braden grunted, as if slightly put out.

"Sorry, honey boy, I don't understand. Do you want to find out this character's name? We can go online. My laptop is in my bedroom. Follow me."

She started away but was stopped by a single word.

"N-no."

She turned around. "Braden. You spoke. Wow. Your dad would be really happy to hear that. But I still don't understand. Do you want to watch the movie? I don't have it, but Gregor probably does."

"No." This time he shook his head, too.

Alex wanted to jump up and down and shout, but she didn't think she should make a big deal about this foray into speech. As if he were a feral kitten and she was coaxing him to eat, she squatted in front of him and said, "Do you know who this character is?"

Braden nodded.

"Can you tell me his name?"

He took a deep breath and opened his mouth, but before

he could say a word, the doorbell rang. Her first thought was her cousin had run something over for Braden, but then Mark appeared in her mind. "Hold that thought, sweetheart. I'd better check in case it's your daddy. Maybe his cell-phone battery died."

She'd tried Mark's number earlier and had been told the cellular customer she was calling wasn't available.

She stood up and started toward the hallway when she felt a small, cool hand touch hers. "Do you want to come?"

Braden nodded.

"Okay. Let's go see who it is."

Out of habit, Alex looked through the peephole before opening the door. A woman in her mid to late fifties was standing on the stoop. A brightly colored wool scarf was wrapped several times around her neck with the ends tucked into her black leather jacket. Her faded blond hair stuck out in wisps not unlike the way Braden's had looked when he'd gotten out of the bath. She was smoking a cigarette, which she dropped to the cement beside the welcome mat and ground out with her heel.

Alex's heart rate sped up. A stranger, but Alex had a suspicion about who this was.

She took Braden's shoulders in her hands and made sure he was looking at her. "Go over by my desk and wait. I don't recognize this person." The bell rang again. "But I don't think she's going away."

After making sure the safety chain was in place, Alex opened the door. "Yes?"

"I'm here for my grandson."

Bingo.

"I'm sorry, but I don't release any child in my care to anyone without a parent's written consent. Please go away."

"And let my grandson stay in the same house as his mother's worst enemy? Not on your life, baby cakes."

Baby cakes? The archaic choice of words almost made Alex smile, but the fact that this woman considered her Tracey's worst enemy wasn't pleasant. She hadn't really *known* Tracey, except by reputation.

She started to close the door, but the woman stuck her arm through the narrow opening and leaned inward. Her breath, which smelled of liquor and cigarettes, was almost enough to make Alex gag.

"You need to leave. Now," she said, as sternly as possible. "Mark will be back soon. If you have a complaint, take it up with him."

"Come here, honey boy," the woman called, making an awkward motion with her hand. "Come to Grandma Odessa."

Alex glanced over her shoulder and saw Braden cover his ears and scoot around the corner of the desk. The look of abject fear in his eyes brought out Alex's fury. She put both hands on the twig-like leather-clad arm and pushed, until the woman let out a yelp and yanked it back.

Leaning her full weight against the door, she closed it firmly and yelled, "Get off my property now before I call the police and file a complaint. If you ever come back, I'll slap a restraining order on you and make sure you spend time in jail."

She could hear the woman's furious reply, but most of the words were unfit for a child's ears so Alex raced to the desk, scooped Braden up in her arms and hurried down the hallway.

She locked the dead bolt on her bedroom door, then grabbed her portable phone and carried Braden to the love seat in her suite area. She made sure he was okay, and then she punched in the first number that came to mind. "Greg, there's someone on my porch. I'll call the police next, but I want you make sure she doesn't try anything while they're coming. Can you—?"

"Hell, yes," he said, not letting her finish the question.

Alex heard him running with the phone. A couple of seconds later, his voice slightly breathless, he said, "Whoever it was is gone. A car took off just as I ran out the door. All I saw was taillights. Couldn't make out the plate. Sorry, cuz."

Alex let out a deep sigh of relief. "No problem. Since I know who it was, I'll give Zeke a jingle, instead of calling 9-1-1. Thanks, Greg. I really appreciate it."

"No problem. The offer still stands. You and the kid can come over here or we can stay with you."

She was more tempted now than she had been earlier, but first she'd see what Zeke had to say. She told Gregor she'd call him back with her decision.

Zeke's cell number was busy, so she turned off the phone and set it on the side table. "Wow," she said, gently brushing the backs of her fingers against Braden's cheek. "That was pretty wild. Your grandmother doesn't take no for an answer, does she?"

Braden looked up—his eyes huge and still filled with worry. Alex's heart shattered, and she had to swallow twice before she could speak. "Braden, I can tell that your grandmother scares you. Heck, she scared me and I'm an adult. I don't like people like that, and I promise I will never let her near you unless you and your dad say it's okay. Do you believe me?"

It took a few seconds before he nodded.

"Good. Now, let me try Zeke again and we—"

The doorbell buzzed.

Braden turned his face into the pillowy cushion of the

An Important Message from the Publisher

Dear Reader,

If you'd enjoy reading contemporary African-American love stories filled with drama and passion, then let us send you two free Kimani Romance™ novels. These books will keep it real with true-to-life African-American characters that turn up the heat and sizzle with passion.

By the way, you'll also get two surprise gifts with your two free books! Please enjoy the free books and gifts with our compliments...

Linda Gill

Publisher, Kimani Press

Peel off Seal and

Place Inside...

We'd like to send you two free books to introduce you to our brand-new line – Kimani Romance™! These novels feature strong, sexy women, and African-American heroes that are charming, loving and true. Our authors fill each page with exceptional dialogue, exciting plot twists, and enough sizzling romance to keep you riveted until the very end!

KIMANI ROMANCE ... LOVE'S ULTIMATE DESTINATION

The Reader Service — Here's How It Works:

sofa, as if hoping it would swallow him whole. "You stay here this time, kiddo. I don't want you to hear what I plan to tell that woman."

Taking the phone with her, Alex hit Redial as she stalked down the hallway. She'd left the lights on in the day care. This time, she didn't even bother to look out the peephole. Forgetting that she'd called Zeke, she planted her feet just opposite the door and shouted, "What is your problem, you stupid woman? What part of 'Go away or I'm calling the police' don't you understand? My mother's boyfriend is a cop. My sister is marrying a cop. My other sister is married to a lawyer. Believe me, this is one family you don't want to mess with."

When no reply was forthcoming, Alex cautiously leaned closer and looked out.

"Zeke," she yelped.

She couldn't get the door opened fast enough. Her fingers felt as if she had ski gloves on. She had to tuck the phone under her arm until she finally got the latch off and the lock undone. "I was just calling—" She made a little cry and whipped the phone out from her armpit. "Sorry," she said sheepishly as she turned it off.

"Not a problem. I was on my way over here when Gregor called. Mark had asked me to drop by and check on things. Are you okay?"

"I am, now. How's Mark? Are you still holding him? Why? You know he didn't kill his wife or anybody else."

"Spoken like a woman defending her man," he said in a kindly way. "He's got a call in to your brother-in-law. Things took a tricky turn. Mark gave the investigators permission to search his house and cars. A gun—the same caliber as the one that killed the drug dealer—turned up in his Nissan."

Alex's stomach rolled and the pain that had been dogging her all day finally let loose a punch that nearly made her bend over. "Whoa, Alex, take it easy. Nobody believes Mark was stupid enough to leave his kid alone in the house while he drove across town and shot the person who was accusing him of murder, then tucked the damn gun under his seat. The gun is a plant. We just have to find the person who put it there."

"Someone who hates Mark enough to try to put him behind bars. Someone like Tracey's mother."

"Yes, I know. I talked to her earlier. Just a hunch, but I think that's how she found out where the little boy was staying. Unfortunately, she has an airtight alibi at the time of death. She was on camera in a blackjack tournament at the Gold Spike. But the lowlife scum she's living with is another possibility. We're looking for him, but so far no luck."

Zeke's obvious belief in Mark's innocence went a long way toward calming Alex's stomach. She looked over her shoulder to make sure Braden wasn't there. "Are Braden and I safe here? Should we go to Greg's?"

"I don't think she'll come back. My guess is she thought she'd take one last chance at bullying you into giving her the kid before she and lover boy took off for Mexico."

The thought of Odessa running off with Braden was almost enough to make Alex sick again.

Zeke put a comforting hand on her shoulder. "Your mother's plane doesn't get in until midnight, but she gave me a key, so I'll be across the street if you need me."

Zeke had her mother's key? The fact surprised her, but Alex decided she was okay with it.

"What about later?" she asked.

He hesitated a moment then said, "I'll be there, then, too. Call if you need us."

Us. "Good," she said, and to her surprise, she meant it.

Chapter Thirteen

The sound of the phone ringing woke Alex from a restless, uneasy sleep filled with images just beyond her reach. She looked at the number on the display. Mark's cell number.

"Hello?"

"Hi. Sorry to wake you."

"No, I'm glad you called," she said, sitting up. The night air was chilly, but her Tweety Bird flannel pajamas kept her from shivering too badly. "Are you still at Metro?"

"Nope. They let me go. My fingerprints didn't match the ones on the gun." He paused then asked, "You heard about that from Zeke, right? He told me you'd talked. I'm really sorry about Odessa. I honestly didn't expect her to show up like that."

"It's okay. We were never in danger." She hoped. "But I did feel badly for Braden. He was pretty shook up."

"Is he asleep?"

"Yeah. Where are you? At home?"

He didn't answer right away. "Actually, I'm out front. They're keeping the Nissan for evidence, and since my truck was here, I had my buddy drop me off. I'm going home, though, and I plan to sleep all day—unless you want me to take Braden with me."

I want you to come in and sleep with me. Terrible idea. Ridiculous. Between her constant low backache and occasional gut-wrenching twinge, she wasn't feeling too alluring. Not to mention the fact that her hormones had turned her into a weepy bundle of nerves.

"No, absolutely not. He's fine here." She got out of bed and walked into the hallway where a tropical-fish nightlight gave her a clear view of Braden's room. His door was partly open and she leaned inside to peek at him.

His covers were a tangled mess, as if he'd been wrestling them—and lost. "He's a restless sleeper, isn't he?"

Mark's low chuckle was sexy even though she knew he didn't intend it to be. "Now, there's an understatement. Usually about this time of night, he starts thrashing and kicking, like he's at war with some horrible demons."

"Night terrors. Fairly common in children his age."

"Do they go away?"

"Yes. Eventually."

Almost as if he'd been waiting for his father's call, Braden started to squirm on the narrow mattress. Eyes squeezed tight, he tossed from one side to the other, moaning. His lips were moving with low, unintelligible cries.

"Uh-oh," Alex murmured.

"I know how to handle this. Can I come in?"

"Of course. Pull in behind my car in the carport and use the side door. I'll meet you there. Will he be okay if I walk away?"

"Yeah, it's just starting. But hurry."

Moments later, Mark brushed past her with a barely murmured greeting or word of thanks. She understood—

and shared—his need for haste. She could hear Braden's cries building.

Mark shucked his leather coat and dropped it on a chair as he rushed to the bed. On his knees, he leaned forward until his head was resting on the pillow beside his son's. "Bray. Bray. It's Daddy. I'm here, son. You're safe. Nobody's gonna hurt you, boy. Nobody. Daddy won't let 'em. Sh…sh… Breathe easy, son. Let it go."

He repeated the phrases over and over while gently stroking the child's forehead whenever Braden stilled enough to allow the touch. Twice, the little boy sat up in bed and looked around, his eyes unseeing. The look of terror on his face was enough to make Alex want to weep, but she didn't. She knelt beside Mark, silently offering her support.

Occasionally, when his shoulders would start to sag, she'd lean over and lightly rub his back. He'd groan softly to let her know the touch was helping, but for the most part Alex was certain her presence was unnoticed by both father and son. This odd ritual seemed to follow a pattern they were familiar with.

After a few long, tense minutes, Braden let out a sigh and fell back against his pillow, eyes closed, mouth lax; his breathing turned shallow, with an occasional exhausted wheeze.

Mark sank back on his heels, head between his arms. Alex longed to hold him and comfort him.

His head tilted sideways and he whispered, "I should have warned you that this might happen, but he hasn't had a nightmare for a few days. I guess I'd hoped he was over them."

She smiled and leaned close to say, "I think we can blame this one on his grandmother. And you handled him well."

Her praise felt good to Mark. So had her nearness and her gentle touch during the ordeal. Watching his son wrestle with his silent demons tore Mark apart. Having someone to share the burden helped beyond anything he could put into words. But he had to try.

Getting to his feet, he found his knees hurt and his ankles were slightly numb. Alex seemed to be suffering from the same affliction because she stumbled against him before catching her balance. Nodding toward the door, he put his arm around her shoulders, and together they hobbled out of the room.

"Damn, I'm getting old," he muttered once they reached the hallway.

"Me, too. My foot was asleep, but I can sure feel it now," she said, bending over to rub her calf. "How long has he been having night terrors?" she asked, looking at him.

In the yellowish glow of the night-light, she looked like a teenager with a tousled bed-head hairdo, oversize pajamas with cartoon characters he remembered from his childhood and an innocent concern that melted his heart. "Except for the past few days, I can only think of two or three nights that he hasn't woken up crying since he came to live with me."

Straightening, she frowned, her sympathy palpable. "I'm glad you were here. I'm not sure I could have given him the same sort of comfort. You really reached deep into the core, I think."

Mark shook his head. "One of the psychologists we saw said Braden is suffering from something so traumatic and deeply ingrained even Braden doesn't know what it is. What he's going through here is his subconscious effort to work it out."

"That sounds logical. He appeared to be trying to say something, but I couldn't understand him."

"I know. His stutter gets even worse under duress. It's

really frustrating. You want to help him so badly and all you can do is comfort him."

She nodded. "I know what you mean."

Her tone held a touch of irony. He was about to ask her to explain, when she took his hand and led him down the hall a few feet and into another room. "I'm tired and you look ready to drop," she said. "How 'bout a cup of cocoa?"

A stiff drink sounded more appropriate given the kind of day he'd had, but he'd sworn off alcohol eight years earlier. He wondered what Alex would say if he told her the reason why he'd quit. "Something hot and sweet sounds good," he said, realizing a second too late how the words could be misconstrued. "If it's no bother."

Her grin told him she'd gotten the inadvertent double entendre. "Instant packets. No work. Have a seat," she said, pointing toward a small nook that was separated from her bedroom by a freestanding curved bookcase.

"Your private abode," he said looking around. Her four-poster bed looked puffy and inviting. A silk duvet in vibrant jewel tones that contrasted with her white sheets. Perfectly Alex. "Very you."

She closed the door of the microwave and pushed a button. "Is that good or bad?" she asked.

"Beautiful. Lavish. Simple. Modern," he said, pointing to the flat-screen television hanging on the wall opposite the love seat. "And traditional."

From the recliner, he picked up the hand-crocheted throw that her mother had given them both as an engagement present. Without stopping to think, he lifted the quilt of vanilla-colored yarn to his face and inhaled. It carried Alex's scent and took his emotions for another dip on the roller coaster.

"We're all complex human beings," she said, turning away to take a second mug from a shelf. "Accumulating baggage as we go through life."

Some visible. Some hidden, he thought.

The bell sounded and she retrieved the cup. She stirred the contents. "Be careful. It's hot," she said, handing it to him. "I'll be back in a second." She smiled. "Or rather, a minute and forty-five seconds."

Their fingers touched in the process of exchanging control of the mug, and her smile vanished. She practically fled back to the safety of her little kitchen.

"You've got a complete home inside a home, don't you?" he observed. "I don't remember this room being so big."

"It wasn't. I added on a couple of years ago. By extending the roofline out, I was able to pick up enough space for what my contractor called my master suite," she said with a chuckle.

With a master bath and its big tub. He didn't say anything, though. There was already something very intimate about this arrangement. He didn't plan on taking it any further. Not that Alex would be interested in hanging out with a guy who'd just spent eight hours being questioned by the police.

When she joined him a few moments later, she settled into the recliner, which was obviously *her* chair, and pulled the knitted comforter over her bare feet. They sipped their cocoa in a companionable silence that Mark knew he could get used to. "I really can't thank you enough for what you've done for me and Braden."

She looked at him over the rim of her mug. Her mumbled "No problem," made him smile.

"My life is nothing but problems," he said. "And I'm

really sorry they've spilled into your lap. You have a business to run and thirty kids to teach tomorrow, and it's after midnight. I should go and let you get to sleep."

He took another drink of cocoa. The chocolate flavor was so rich and sweet it transported him to a blissful world and made him miss what she said to him.

"Wait. Back up. I'm a little punchy. Did you just ask me to stay here tonight?"

She nodded, a blush coloring her cheeks. "There's a pullout bed in Braden's room. Then you'll be close if he wakes up again."

A nice offer, but not the arrangement he would have chosen—if things had been different between them. "Trust me, he's out for the count. I wish I could say the same in my case, but I'm usually awake for another hour or so after one of these episodes. It would be probably be better if I went home. That way you and Braden can both sleep without me bothering you."

Alex knew his plan was the smart one. Let him go. Turn off the lights and crawl into her big empty bed and try to forget all the feelings that had been building between them. But she couldn't.

She set her mug on the little table beside her remote control and curled her feet under herself. "Mark, what if you stayed…here…with me."

There, I said it. Oh, God, I said it.

His dark brows rose in question. "Are you serious?"

His obvious disbelief did nothing for her self-confidence. She'd slept with other men since Mark's defection, but there hadn't been anyone in almost a year. Still, she didn't remember the "I want to sleep with you" talk as this humiliating.

"We don't have to have sex. We don't even have to get under the covers. Well, I do," she qualified. "You know I like to be warm and cozy when I sleep. But today's been really horrible, and I think we both could use some comfort. Don't you?"

"Comfort," he murmured, his expression slowly changing to one of comprehension. "You want someone to cuddle with. I got it. Sure. No problem."

He didn't understand. Not really. Heck, she wasn't sure she could explain the urge propelling her back into the arms of the man who'd once broken her heart so badly, but her Gypsy sixth-sense told her she needed to be with him tonight.

Chapter Fourteen

Mark watched the woman he'd once loved with all his heart rinse out the two mugs then turn to face him. "Besides, it's not like we're strangers. We used to sleep together all the time. Remember how scandalized my dad was when I moved in with you?"

Her impish smile sealed his fate. He remembered. He remembered carrying her over the threshold—even though she'd protested that she weighed too much and that he'd put his back out.

"Where's the bathroom? I'd like to wash up."

"Of course. The guest bath is across the hall from Braden's room. I keep extra toothbrushes in the drawer in case my sisters wind up spending the night."

Her sisters? Or men friends? *Like I have any business asking,* he silently scolded. He'd dated a few women after his divorce, but none of the relationships had led to anything. He was far too wary of being fooled again. Tracey had pretended to be one person, when in reality she was someone very different. Unlike Alex, he thought. With Alex, there was no deceit. She was who she was.

And she was already in bed when he returned. He'd

removed his long-sleeved T-shirt, grateful for the white, V-neck undershirt beneath it. He took off his belt and undid the button on his jeans, then kicked off his shoes and sat down on the bed. "I could grab that throw and sleep on top of the covers."

She'd turned off the lights in the sitting room and kitchenette, making it too dark for him to read her gaze. But he saw her smile. "We're grown-ups, Mark. We can do what we want. If you want to sleep on top of the covers, you may. But I'd prefer to have you under here with me."

Oh, God. He took off his socks then his jeans. Since the collar of her pajamas was visible above the edge of the covers she'd drawn up to her chin, he kept his underwear on and crawled between the sheets.

Cool enough to make him inhale sharply, but these were high-quality linens. Soft and inviting. The featherbed mattress topper made him feel as if he'd slipped into a cocoon. A long, satisfied sigh followed. "I know this sounds strange, but this feels like coming home."

Alex turned on her side to look at him. "I'm glad. Shall I turn the light off?"

"In a minute. Can I ask you something first?"

Her sigh held a curious note that startled him. "What is it about sleepovers that makes people share their deepest, darkest secrets? My sisters are the same way. Whenever we'd sleep together, we'd talk half the night."

He smiled. "You can tell me your deepest, darkest secret if you want, but I was just wondering if I should set the alarm on my watch or will yours go off before seven? I'll need to drive Braden to school since he's not set up to ride the bus from here."

Her chuckle turned into a giggle. "That's funny. My

mother would be appalled by my inability to read your mind." Sitting up, she turned off the bedside lamp and said, "My alarm goes off at five-forty-five. Which is not very far away. Good night."

He smiled and waited for his eyes to grow accustomed to the dark. Enough light angled through the slats of the blinds in her window that he could make out her profile. He turned on his side and inched a little closer. "I thought my purpose here was to provide snuggling. I can't do that with you all the way over there."

She made a happy sound and wiggled closer. The sheets shifted out of the way and suddenly they were touching. Their toes and feet were the only bare skin that met, but even that little bit of contact set Mark's imagination on fire. When he breathed in, her scent filled his senses—indescribable in its subtlety but something uniquely Alex.

After a momentary awkwardness, he managed to get his arm out so her head could rest on his bicep. "Don't flex," she said. "You could put a kink in my neck."

He laughed outright. "Was that a compliment?"

"Well, you are pretty buff compared to when we were dating."

"Do you know how much a fire hose weighs?"

She shook her head.

"A lot. Actually, the physicality of the job is something I miss since I went into arson, although I still take part in trainings whenever I can because I could get called in to work a fire if we were shorthanded."

"You probably never knew this," she said softly. "But I've always had a thing for firemen."

Her hair tickled his neck. When he brushed the errant lock aside, he accidentally touched her forehead. Her skin was velvety soft and once he started touching her, he found he couldn't stop.

His fingertips traveled over her brow, her cheeks and her lips—which turned up. "Are you practicing Braille?" she quipped.

"Just exploring the terrain. Would you rather I didn't?"

She didn't answer right away. "Can I touch, too?"

The question was low and sexy and made his body respond like a teen on his first date. She didn't wait for an answer. Instead, she turned all the way on her side and put her hand flat on his chest.

Knowing she could probably feel the thudding of his heart made him nearly as embarrassed as he was horny. "Alex, you're starting something you might not want to finish."

It wasn't a question. It was an out, she realized. And she loved him for it. But her mind was made up. She wanted more than comfort, more than snuggling. She wanted escape.

She planted a row of kisses along the scratchy growth of his lower jaw. She'd forgotten to tell him about the disposable razors in the drawer. "We've talked enough." Unless there was some other reason why they shouldn't have sex. "I have condoms in the drawer, and I had a full range of blood tests done a few months ago when I was in the hospital. Is there something health-wise I need to know about?"

"No. That wasn't what I meant. But given our histories—and your family—are you sure this is a good thing?"

She pushed herself up to rest her chest against his. Although the room was dark, there was light enough to see his features. He was worried. She didn't blame him. Her father had once threatened to toss him to her cousins and let them beat him within an inch of his life. Not that Ernst would have done that, but he'd been furious on her behalf after learning of Mark's cheating.

She outlined his lips with her fingertip. "If memory serves me correctly," she said, going for seductive, "*this* was a very, very good thing when we were together."

His chuckle stopped when he put his hand behind her head and drew her down for a kiss. A powerful, full-of-heat kiss that blocked almost every thought from her head. Fleetingly she remembered that she wasn't taking birth-control pills, but that wasn't really an issue. The pains she'd experienced off and on all day were the type she remembered as premenstrual. Besides, this wasn't the right time of the month to get pregnant.

"I'll mostly be working from memory," he said, trailing kisses down the open neckline of her pajamas. "I haven't been with a woman in six months or more, but I have the results of a recent AIDS test in my locker at work, if you'd like to see it."

"Why'd you get tested?"

"Part of the new life-insurance policy I took out after Tracey died. For Braden."

That gesture as much as anything made her dizzy with love. "You're a good man, Mark Gaylord. Now, shut up and make love to me."

And he did. No questions asked.

Well, one. "Do these pajama bottoms have a drawstring?"

"Oh, sorry," she said, lifting her hips so she could pluck at the cotton ribbon she'd hastily tied hours earlier.

Once the knot was undone, she tugged down the voluminous flannel pants and kicked free of them. She was about to remove her top, which Mark had already unbuttoned, when she felt his hands on her waist. His fingers flayed in a fanlike gesture that covered her belly. Her poor scarred belly.

"Alex," he said sharply. "What's this?"

"Oh, um, I had an operation."

He rolled over and reached for the bedside lamp.

"No, Mark, don't. It's ugly. Can't you just pretend it's not there?"

He paused but turned on the light a second later. "Why would I do that? It's part of you."

She yanked the covers up to her chin. One minute she'd felt sexy and wanton, the next ugly and deformed. "Not a part I'm proud of."

Frowning, he pried loose her grip on the sheets. Instead of flinging them back, he said, "What happened? Were you in an accident?"

Just tell the man and be done with it, she told herself. "I had a laparoscopy procedure, which involves making two small incisions and looking inside my abdomen with a telescope thing. My doctor was removing a cyst on one of my fallopian tubes. Afterward I wound up with an infection and was back in the hospital on IV antibiotics a week later. Some of the tissue around the incision died, and I had to have another operation to fix that."

He lowered the sheet and carefully, lovingly parted the two halves of her pajama top. "When?" he asked, gently running his index finger over the scars.

"About a year after we split up."

"Poor baby. I didn't know. I'm so sorry."

"It wasn't your fault. I've always had 'female problems,' as my aunt used to say. I was in a lot of pain each month, so my doctor suggested surgery. When he got inside and looked around, he couldn't believe such a small cyst was responsible for so much pain, so he poked around a bit more than necessary. This made my recovery more difficult."

"Is everything okay now?"

How much to share…? "Pretty much. As long as I take high-dose birth-control pills so that my body doesn't ovulate. That lowers the chance of new cysts forming."

He didn't say anything for a minute then he sighed. "After we got engaged, you went off the pill. You thought we should get pregnant right away—while we were young enough to be cool parents."

He looked so troubled and guilty; she touched his cheek and smiled. "I could have started taking the pill again after we broke up, but I was so busy setting up this place, moving out of your apartment…I just didn't pay much attention to my health. The pain was more an annoyance than anything else, and I honestly never thought twice about the pros and cons of having the cyst removed. I just wanted it done so I could get back to my life."

"And it ended up nearly costing you your life," he said. "Oh, Alex, I wish I'd known. I hate the thought of you going through that without me."

He kissed her belly, tenderly tracing the raised white ridges with his lips. "But you know we all have scars. Some are just more visible than others."

Alex's heart discovered a healing truth in his words—and touch. She sat up and shrugged off her top. "You're right," she said. "I've shown you mine. Your turn, tough guy."

Mark had to say something. But what? He had scars galore, but none that compared to the divot that been taken from her belly.

He flopped on his back and held up his right hand. He made a fist and cocked his wrist so she could see his skin.

"Remember this line? You asked me about it once when we first started dating. I told you I was teasing my pet dog and he scratched me. You believed me, didn't you?"

She touched her finger to the thin white line. "Of course. Why wouldn't I?"

They both knew why she might not trust him now, but back then her love had been pure and uncorrupted—unlike anything else in his life. "Well, what I told you was a lie. I never had a pet dog in my life. My dad wouldn't allow it. This scar and probably half a dozen others came from him."

"Oh," she said, shaking her head. "That's so sad. Why didn't you tell me?"

"Because I thought you'd think less of me for it. Your family was perfect. If your dad would have known about the kind of man my father was, he'd have found a way to ship me off to Timbuktu."

"No, he wouldn't have. I wouldn't have let him."

He snickered softly. "I know. But I wasn't used to having someone else fighting on my side. Everything happened so fast between us—we met, fell in love, moved in together, got engaged and bought a house. I think at some level I knew I'd eventually blow it…and I did."

"We *both* blew it, Mark. I knew you were nervous about how fast things were progressing between us, but when I have an agenda…look out. Just ask my sisters," she said with a soft snicker. "When we used to dance as the Sisters of the Silver Dollar, I was a real diva. We wore the costumes I picked out, did the numbers I wanted. I swear that's one of the reasons we stopped performing together. That, and Dad's death."

She sighed deeply and sat up. "Life has a way of teaching us lessons we need to learn. I still like to run things…

obviously, but now I try to listen to other opinions, too. So, if you're more comfortable with a pillow between us tonight, I say, 'No problem.'"

She leaned sideways to pick up the full-length body pillow she sometimes slept with.

Mark looked at it then let out a groan. "I don't think so." He pulled it from her grasp and sent it flying. Then he kissed her with passion so familiar, so well-remembered, it was as if their years apart had never happened.

Later, satiated and complete, she snuggled against him. One errant thought crossed her mind. *We forgot to use a condom.* She tensed for a moment then let out a sigh. *Oh, well. My PMS should mean no chance of getting pregnant.* Plus, her doctor had told her it might take months before her body was back to normal and she could try in vitro. Conceiving a child tonight would border on the miraculous.

Chapter Fifteen

Alex woke up before her alarm went off. She slid out of bed, being careful not to disturb Mark, who was asleep. On his belly. One hand curled under the pillow.

When they'd first been together—in his early years in the police force, she'd teased him about keeping a gun in that hand. He'd never denied it, but she'd known it wasn't true. Even then, she'd had a sense that he wasn't a cop at heart.

She gathered the clothes she'd set out to wear today, then showered and dressed in the spare bathroom, which afforded more privacy and was less likely to wake Mark. After checking on Braden, who looked as peaceful and serene as his father, she went into the day care's kitchen and made coffee.

Rita and the two younger aides would be arriving soon. Alex's lesson-plan book was open on the desk. She'd made sure the day's craft project was set up the night before. Over in the story nook, the felt-covered easel was waiting for her reading-readiness lesson. The casual observer might think her day—her life—was well organized and on track.

But they'd be wrong. Inside, her stomach was a ball of nerves, her mind was bouncing all over the place and she had a dreadful fear she might break down and cry if some-one said the wrong thing.

Hormones, she told herself. And lack of sleep.

She poured a mug of coffee then walked back to her private rooms to wake up the person responsible for her missed hours of rest. *What have I done? Where do we go from here?* The last question, she realized, was her big-gest concern.

She and Mark had made love. The old feelings that they'd cautiously avoided these past weeks had come back full force. The sex was just as hot as she remembered. They cared about each other—deeply. But neither had mentioned the word *love*. Which made sense considering how crazy their lives were at the moment.

We need to step back, she decided. *Take it slow. We can be friends. Our relationship should be professional. I'm his child's teacher. He's a client. Yes,* she told herself firmly, *that is the only way to handle this situation.*

"Good morning," she said, closing her bedroom door behind her.

"In here," a deep, husky voice called from her bathroom. "I didn't think you'd want me running down the hallway in my Skivvies, so I used your shower. Hope that was okay."

The door was partly open. She went closer, not sure *she* was ready to see him in his Skivvies. "Of course. I brought you a cup of coffee."

"Thanks. Come on in. I'm decent."

The steamy, man-scented air made her knees wobble. She wasn't used to sharing her space with another person—especially someone so…masculine. And desirable.

"Here."

"Um…" he said, taking the cup from her. "Smells great."

He took a drink then put it on the counter to finger comb his still-wet hair. "Is Bray up?"

"No. I thought I'd let you do the honors—in case he's disoriented. Plus, it will do him good to see you. He was pretty worried about you last night."

"Did he tell you that?"

"No, but I could tell."

His smile was friendly and teasing. "Your Gypsy mind-reading abilities kicking in?"

"My years of teaching."

"Oh." He reached out and took her arm, drawing her closer. "Is it time?"

She resisted for half a second. "Time for what?"

"The morning-after talk. You're regretting last night."

He knew her well. "Not exactly. It's just that we both have our hands full at the moment, and embarking on a new relationship—"

"Or rekindling an old one," he put in.

"Right. Well, either one probably isn't a smart thing. Maybe after the holidays…when things slow down, we can reevaluate how we feel—"

His sharp laugh took her by surprise. His eyes narrowed and he shook his head. "I know how I feel, Alex. The same way I felt when I asked you to marry me. *That* never changed, even though I tried to pretend it had. Tracey knew the truth. Why do you think she hated you so much?"

"I…I didn't know she did. At least, until Odessa told me."

"Oh, yeah. We fought about you all the time. One of the many marriage counselors we saw said that in Tracey's mind you were a living ghost. No matter what I did, she never believed that I loved her more than you. And do you know why?"

Alex shook her head.

"Because I didn't. God knows I tried, but I couldn't. You were—you are—the one, Alex."

He made it sound simple. And, deep in her heart, Alex knew the same was true for her, but she couldn't say the words. Not now. Not when she finally had her life in order.

Mark's sigh brought her attention back to him. "But, I wasn't any great prize nine years ago when we met. Your father was quick to point that out—and he was right. Now, my life is even more out of whack. A psycho ex-mother-in-law who terrorizes people in the middle of the night. A job that I'm in danger of losing. A kid who's probably completely screwed up because of his mother and me." He made a caustic sound. "So, if you're here to ask me to leave, I will."

"Last night was…well, it felt too good to be true. Just like before. That sort of fairy tale–destiny thing, but, Mark, I don't trust that anymore. If we couldn't make what was between us work when we had it easy, then how can we expect to succeed now?"

"You're absolutely right. And you deserve better, Alex. That's why I never called you after Tracey and I split up. I failed you once, and I'm not going to put you through that again. Since the meth-lab fire is still under investigation, I can't work. Since I'm not working, there's no reason for Braden to keep coming here. If things ever go back to normal after the first of the year, we'll make other day-care arrangements."

There was more to say, but the sound of her employees entering the building told her she needed to cut this discussion short. But she wasn't about to let her personal life create any additional trauma for Braden.

"No," she said sternly. "I mean, yes—you and me. We

should step back. Think about how to handle this. We have enough stress in our lives without…" She realized she was rambling, repeating her doctor's orders. "But we can't let this affect Braden. He needs his routine. He's comfortable here. He's made friends—Maya and Luca adore him. That's a big deal at this age and a giant personal step for your son. Let him continue to come here—at least until we close for the holiday break."

"P-pul-please, D-D-Daddy."

Alex spun around. Braden was standing a foot away, completely dressed and ready for school. His hair was sticking up in places and his shirt wasn't tucked in, but he had his backpack in one hand and his coat in the other.

Alex moved aside so Mark could reach his son. "Hey, Bray. I didn't see you there, bud. Miss Alex and I were having a talk. I wasn't sure we should come back here after what Grandma Odessa did last night. She shouldn't have come here, Braden. It's against the rules that the judge set up to keep you safe. I didn't think it was fair to put Miss Alex in the middle of our problems."

Miss Alex. The name made her want to cry, but she understood why he was using it—to distance himself and Braden from the mistake Alex and he had made.

"And like I told your dad," Alex said, "I appreciate the offer, but it's not your fault your grandmother doesn't follow the rules. I really hope you can continue to come here, at least until school lets out for the holiday break."

"Alexandra?" a familiar voice called from the hallway. "Your students are arriving."

"Mom?" Her mother had returned from her whirlwind trip to Detroit so late Alex hadn't expected to see her this morning. "I have to go," she said, stepping away from

Mark. "I'm sure what your father decides will be for the best, but Braden, if I don't see you later, have a happy Christmas, okay?"

She gave the little boy a hug and ran from the room, praying her ever-observant mother wouldn't see her unshed tears.

Three hours later, after a rousing rendition of "Jingle Bells"—complete with fourteen pairs of sleigh bells, Alex was outdoors supervising the play yard. She was pushing the M&M's, as she privately called Maya, Morgan, Madelaine and MacKensie, on the swings while the rest of her students wore off a little pent-up energy on other jungle-gym equipment.

Every year the craziness of the holiday season seemed to get worse, even though she did her best to keep the more commercial aspects out of the classroom. Her students read books that celebrated the various religious traditions that took place in the final weeks of December. She used the arrival of the solstice to study the planets and seasons. Many of her stories and lessons stressed the joy of giving, but still, the frenetic buildup to *the big day* slipped into everyone's life.

"I wanna Snowboard Barbie, a My Little Pony barn and a new bike," Morgan announced.

MacKensie's list of must-haves was twice as long, and Maddie was making a valiant effort to top it.

Alex hoped Santa was listening—because she wasn't. Not really. She couldn't stop thinking about Braden and Mark. What if Odessa tried to steal Braden from his school?

"You could call him."

Alex startled. She hadn't heard her mother approach. "Mom. You know I hate it when you sneak up on me," she said sharply, giving MacKensie another push.

Maya, who was dragging the toes of her glossy black

Mary Janes in the sand beneath her swing, tossed back her head, giggling. "Gramma was standing there a long time, Auntie Alex. Didn't you see her?"

Alex felt her face heat up. "I guess not, sweetie. Sometimes mothers can make themselves invisible. That's how they know when their kids do something wrong."

The other little girls' eyes went wide. "She's teasing," Maya reassured them. "Let's go play with Parker and Preston."

All four girls jumped off their swings and raced across the yard to the slide area.

Alex's mother followed them with her gaze and sighed. "Don't you wish you had a little of that energy?"

"What's that supposed to mean?" Alex snapped, immediately regretting her snarly tone.

"Did someone not get enough sleep?"

"Someone slept fine." For the few hours when she'd closed her eyes. "Someone has a lot on her mind." The part she wasn't in the process of losing. "How did you sleep? Or should I ask, with whom did you sleep?"

Yetta's eyebrows lifted in surprise then she smiled. "That sounds like something Grace would have said in an attempt to deflect attention away from her guilty conscience."

Alex agreed. She normally wasn't testy or defensive, but, then, she usually didn't have anything to be testy or defensive about. "Sorry. I assume Zeke told you about our crazy night, but that's no reason to take it out on you. Especially considering you're here volunteering when you're probably still on Detroit time. How was Grace and everybody?"

Yetta put an arm around Alex's shoulders and squeezed. "Now, that attempt at changing the subject was much more like the Alexandra we all know and love."

"Mom, why don't you use anyone's nickname?"

"Stubbornness. Your father and I chose each of our daughter's names with care. If I'd wanted you to be called Alex, I could have named you that. Instead, we chose Alexandra, after your father's great-great-grandmother."

"Really?" Alex said in surprise. "I thought I was named after some famous Russian princess or czarina or whatever the heck she was."

"A myth your father encouraged sometime after Katherine's birth, I believe. Someone—possibly Claude—mentioned noticing a certain underlying pattern to your names, and Ernst jumped on the idea."

"Why?"

"To bolster your self-esteem. Our heritage is so often poorly portrayed by the media and in movies. He had many negative experiences while growing up—early cases of racial profiling, you might say. Ernst felt that if you thought of yourself as princesses, you would stand proud in the face of any teasing you might encounter."

"What about the story he told us of his ancestor who fell in love with a prince and had his baby?"

Yetta pursed her lips. "Who knows? It could have happened. The Romani were never big on written records."

"And most were creative storytellers, like Dad."

Alex checked her watch. The sunny day begged more play time, but they still had a number of things that needed to get done today. She blew her whistle and watched her students race to the door and form a shaky line.

"Alexandra," her mother called when Alex was a few steps away.

"Yes?"

"One of your father's great-aunts back east had a painting of the first Alexandra, the woman who was supposed to have loved the prince. She was very beautiful. In fact, she looked a lot like you. It's not surprising that a man would risk everything to be with her—even if society deemed that such a union was wrong."

Alex wondered if there was some underlying message in her mother's comment, but she pushed the thought away. She needed to stay in the present. Her students required her attention, and doing her job was what paid her bills.

MARK HAD BEEN GRATEFUL to get Zeke's call shortly after dropping Braden off at school. He'd walked the boy inside to explain the situation about his son's grandmother to the principal then returned to his truck, without any real direction or purpose.

He'd just made up his mind to return to his apartment and watch television when his cell phone had rung.

"I'm headed to a stakeout. Wanna come?" Zeke asked. "As a very unofficial observer."

Mark hadn't hesitated. "Hell, yes."

"I'll pick you up at your place in thirty minutes."

That had been four hours ago. Since that time, they'd driven to Searchlight, a small, dusty oasis about fifty miles south of Vegas. Directly east was Lake Mojave, where Mark recalled relaxing on a houseboat that summer when he and Alex had been dating. As tempting as it was to linger over those memories—especially after spending the night in Alex's arms—he narrowed his focus to the two-story dump of a motel where Odessa and her boyfriend were supposedly holed up.

He took a drink of the bitter, lukewarm coffee he'd picked up at the casino a few blocks down the street.

A quick glance at his watch told him Alex's preschool class was probably just ending. Parents would be lined up to greet their kids, oohing and aahing over the latest masterpiece their progeny had produced. Braden had missed out on that whole experience.

Alex had been right when she'd said Braden was showing signs of improvement since he'd started attending the Dancing Hippo. On the way to school that morning, he'd actually said a few words instead of grunting or shrugging his shoulders. The stutter was still pronounced, but, at least, he was trying, Mark thought.

Which is why he should continue to go there, even if Alex and I can't figure out this thing between us.

As if tapping into Mark's private thoughts, his companion behind the wheel said, "I saw your truck parked behind Alex's this morning. Something I should know about?"

"Maybe if you were her father."

The snide remark landed between them like a loaded gun.

Zeke let out a wry chuckle. "Good point."

Mark sank a little lower in the seat. "No. That was a stupid thing to say. Seems to be the only thing coming out of my mouth lately. I know you care about Yetta and her family. You have a right. More of a right than I do, actually."

"I wouldn't say that."

"Well, it's true. If Ernst were alive, he'd have been waiting at my tailgate this morning with a cup of coffee and a baseball bat."

"Really? Why?"

Mark grinned. "'Cause he always liked coffee in the morning—strong and black. And the bat was a great intimidator. Not that I ever saw him use it."

Zeke rubbed the side of his nose and let out a sigh.

"Ever since I started seeing Yetta, I've been hearing stories like that. The Gypsy King was larger than life. Like Elvis. He's never quite left the building, if you get my drift."

"Yeah. I understand. Even eight years later, I kinda feel like he's looking over my shoulder, scowling. He didn't have too many good things to say about me."

"How come? First time I met you, I knew you were a square shooter."

Mark appreciated the comment, but for all of Zeke's cop instincts and years of experience, he was still basically trusting—at least where his brethren in law enforcement were concerned. "Alex once told me that in the old days the Rom men were the ones with the special abilities to see into the future and stuff. They were the original horse whisperers."

Zeke nodded, listening. "Go on."

"At some point, that changed. I don't know why, but the women became the ones who read tea leaves and looked into crystal balls. Telling the future became a commercial enterprise. The men still had these gifts, but they forgot how to use them."

"Oh…" Zeke said. "You mean Ernst could see things about you that most people couldn't."

"Right. The first time Alex brought me to the house for dinner, he said, 'You know that adage about the apple not falling far from the tree? Well, what they don't say is that the apple is bruised, and no good to eat.'"

Zeke didn't say anything, but Mark saw his hands tighten around the wheel.

"I sorta laughed it off, but what he said stuck with me a long time. When Tracey told me she was pregnant, I decided Ernst was right. If I had a daughter, I wouldn't want her stuck with spoiled fruit, either."

Zeke punched the steering wheel. "That's crap. You're a decent man who made a mistake and afterward did the right thing—the honorable thing. Even Yetta admits that Ernst was way off base where you were concerned." That was news to Mark. "I wish to hell I had a damn baseball bat. I'd—"

His rant was cut short by the cackle of a two-way radio. The backup unit was checking in. The second car had already been in place when Zeke and Mark had arrived and was positioned around back in case the suspects tried to slip out on foot.

Zeke confirmed that nothing was happening but ordered the pair to hold off sending one of the two for food. "Check-out time is one. I'll have the front desk call the room to rattle their cage."

He made a call on his cell phone then sat up, leaning over the steering wheel. Dropping his chin, he looked at Mark and said, "You know my daughter just had a baby, right?"

Mark nodded. Zeke had returned from Los Angeles, where his ex-wife and daughter lived, with a two-inch stack of photos. Mark had never seen his friend more energized. "Well, seeing her and this tiny new life made me realize that everything that happened in the past is gone. It's done. We can't change it and we can never really make up for it. We just have to deal with what's going on now."

"That's pretty deep coming from you."

Zeke's hand shot out but the punch Mark expected didn't come. Instead, he tapped Mark's shoulder softly and said, "I'm a grandpa, now. I'm entitled. I just don't want you to throw away something good because you feel guilty about letting Alex down in the past. If I'd done that, I wouldn't have been there to hold the most beautiful little grandbaby in the world. Did I show you her picture?"

Mark roared, knowing Zeke was trying to lighten the moment. "Yeah, I've see her picture. But what about you, Dr. Phil? Do you just give advice or do you follow your own?"

Zeke's smile turned into a scowl. "My case is different."

"How?"

"Yetta isn't Alex. She was married for thirty-plus years—to a freakin' icon, thank you very much. You try competing with the Gypsy King, and then we'll talk."

"I have, and I lost," Mark said. "Sure, Yetta married the man, but Alex worshipped him. She was Daddy's little princess. And even though Ernst never said the exact words to my face, I knew he was thinking, 'Oh, God, what a loser. That boy is nothing but trouble.' Which is exactly what my father always said. So, of course, I had to go and prove him right."

"You made a mistake. And part of that was Tracey's fault. You think Ernst never made a mistake?"

"Not a life-changing whopper, like mine."

Zeke didn't speak for a moment, but when he did, his voice was low and serious. "Well, you're wrong. I don't know how much Alex knows, but Grace uncovered a pretty dark secret about her dad when she was helping us nail that lowlife scum Charles Harmon."

"What kind of secret?"

"The Gypsy King broke the law. He took a bribe, and instead of giving half to the man who'd arranged it—ol' Chucky boy—he kept the whole thing. Put the money into mutual funds for his daughters."

Mark's jaw dropped. "The money Alex used as her part of the down payment on the Hippo was illicit?"

"The seed money was. Apparently over the years, the trusts did very well. And there was never any complaint filed. The money came from some deep pockets behind one of the unions. We only have Harmon's word on this. So, it's never going to be made public."

"Does Yetta know?"

Zeke nodded.

"Wow. That's wild. I swear I thought the man walked on water."

"Well, he wasn't perfect, but that doesn't mean his family loves him any less."

Mark heard something in his friend's tone and realized the same truth applied to Zeke and the daughter he'd reconciled with a few months earlier. "So, tell me again. Why are you waffling about dating Yetta?"

"Because I'm old, dammit. I'm getting ready to retire. What does someone like Yetta want with a gray-haired bum sitting around all day?"

"Who said you have to sit around? Let me ask you something. Say that nutcase boyfriend of my ex-wife's mother's blows out that door with a loaded 410 and puts a hole in your chest. Whose face are you going to see in your mind before you disappear into the light—or wherever you're headed?"

Zeke's growl didn't include a name, but Mark knew whose name would be on his lips when it was his time. *Alex*. But what if the best thing he could do for her was leave her alone? She had a good life. She didn't need the kind of bull that seemed to follow wherever he went. She deserved a sweet, unblemished apple.

A minute later, the second-floor door that they'd been watching opened. Two people walked out. A short, skinny man wearing a black cowboy hat, a soiled-looking denim jacket and sloppy jeans badly in need of a belt. The woman was dressed in shiny pink exercise pants and a fuzzy fake fur jacket that didn't quite cover her sagging behind. There was no mistaking the fact that this was a May-December romance, but the way Odessa tugged on the younger man's arm told Mark who was running the show.

The cowboy seemed to be having a little trouble walking. "Stoned?" Mark asked.

"High on something," Zeke murmured. He let their backup know that the subjects of their stakeout were moving, then he nodded at Mark to get out of the car.

The pair paid them no mind as they stumbled toward a beat-up Ford Mustang parked just a few cars away from Zeke's unmarked patrol car.

Mark was unarmed, but he wasn't worried. Odessa obviously had her hands full with lover boy, who might have had a gun under his bulky jacket but probably couldn't see past his nose to aim and shoot.

"Odessa Mapes, LVMPD," Zeke barked. "We need to talk."

The pair froze. For a moment, Mark thought they might run, but the appearance of two uniformed officers took away some of their options. That didn't keep Odessa from dropping her hold on her companion and advancing on Mark with her usual bluster.

"You," she shrieked. "You cowardly piece of shit. What my worthless daughter ever saw in you—beyond a regular paycheck—is beyond me. I tried to talk her out of marrying you, but would she listen? Hell, no."

Mark had heard the same recriminations and complaints for every year of his marriage—and after his divorce, too. Practically from the moment Mark and his mother-in-law had been introduced—after his and Tracey's quickie wedding—

Odessa had groused about him. "He's too controlling, too hard, too cold-blooded." The list had grown over the years.

"These gentlemen from Metro are here to take you in, Odessa. A small matter of a handgun that was found in my car, without my fingerprints on it. A gun that was used to kill the guy who supposedly named me as a murder suspect in your daughter's death."

Her companion let out a keening moan and started muttering something about Mexico. He was swaying on his feet so badly the backup team had to each take an arm while Zeke cuffed him.

Zeke rattled off the man's rights and made him answer out loud that he understood. "Uh, yeah, sure. Whatever."

His chin dropped to his chest, but a second later his head snapped back so hard his hat fell off. As the officers started helping him to the police unit, he began to struggle. "Wait. Odey," he called to the woman standing a foot from Mark. "Baby, you're not gonna let 'em take me in, are you? I thought we were going to Mexico, 'member?"

Odey? The coffee in Mark's stomach curdled slightly.

"Wait. Hold on, man. I gotta see. I gotta see which one is the dumb f—" The cop on the left jerked the man around, slurring the rest of his obvious epithet.

"Wait," Zeke ordered the officer. To the suspect, he asked, "What do you want to see?"

"Which one is he, Odey? That dude? Is he the one who *thinks* he's the brat's dad?"

Odessa let out a string of swear words and would have inflicted bodily harm on the man if Zeke hadn't held her back. "Not yet, you fool," she shrieked. "Not till we get the money."

Mark and Zeke looked at each other. "What money?"

She turned to face Mark. Her rheumy eyes were narrowed with spite and she practically spit the words at him. "The money you're gonna pay me to keep quiet about who Braden's real father is."

Chapter Sixteen

In the week following Alex and Mark's morning-after talk, Alex saw very little of Mark. He'd continued to allow Braden to attend the Dancing Hippo, but only put in an appearance himself at the end of the day when he picked up his son.

He was polite but distant. Alex thought he looked tired—defeated—but she was never given a chance to ask him anything personal. He made sure they were never alone.

Alex had worried that the tension between his teacher and his father would cause Braden to regress. Fortunately, that wasn't the case. Although his stutter was still very pronounced, the little boy was slowly opening up—even speaking in the company of his friends, who never rushed or teased him.

When he wasn't sequestered in some corner with Maya and Gemilla, Braden played video games with Luca. And she'd even seen Luca helping the younger boy with his math problems.

Braden was a smart kid—from the simple tests she'd put him through, she'd determined that he was on par with his grade level in math and even slightly above grade level in reading—but he rarely volunteered answers to the questions she'd ask him about the books he carried in his backpack. And when he did speak, his stutter broke her heart.

But she'd noticed today that his little brow seemed less furrowed, as if some weight had been lifted from his shoulders. Alex wondered if something had changed in school, maybe some accomplishment she wasn't aware of.

"Braden, you're smiling again," Alex said, catching his hand as he passed by her desk on his way to join Maya at the snack table. He came to her willingly, but he didn't crawl up on her lap as most of the children in her school would have. "Can you tell me why you're so happy? Is it because Christmas is only five days away?"

He shook his head. "N-no m-ore…G-Grandma."

Something had happened with Odessa? That *was* good news. Zeke had mentioned that the woman had been picked up, but he hadn't elaborated and Alex hadn't asked. She saw Mark every day. Shouldn't he be the one to tell her what was going on?

"Did the judge tell her not to come here anymore?"

He shook his head from side to side.

"Did she move away?"

He nodded.

Thank God. She made a mental note to ask Mark when he came to pick up Braden.

As usual, the last two hours of her workday disappeared in a blur. She was more exhausted than usual and could barely keep her eyes open when six o'clock rolled around. *A week of no sleep will do that to a person,* she told herself.

Lately, her dreams teeter-tottered back and forth between a rosy picture of what her future might hold if she let Mark back in to share it and nightmares that featured a wicked grandmother carting a child off into the woods.

Occasionally there were sexy dreams, too. Memories really. And she found the thought of spending the rest of her days without that kind of fire in her life utterly depressing.

"Ahem."

Alex looked up from her keyboard where her fingers were resting lifelessly. "Mark. I didn't hear you come in."

His eyebrows framed a question. *How is that possible?* She didn't have an answer, so she stood up and said, "I'm glad you're here. I wanted to ask you a question. Braden told me his grandmother was no longer a problem. Could you explain?"

"Odessa is in county lockup for a fistful of speeding tickets and unpaid parking fines while the D.A. decides if there's enough evidence to charge her with accessory to murder."

"What?" she asked, trying to keep her voice under a shout. "Didn't Zeke say she had an alibi?"

"Her boy-toy cowboy—" He winced apologetically. "Sorry. That's what the jokers at Metro call him. He's actually a forty-year-old druggie who has the IQ of a Barbie doll when he's not high. Once he started coming down from whatever drug cocktail Odessa was feeding him, he claimed that she put him up to it."

"Wow. No more threat of her stealing Braden. You must be overjoyed." Although she had to admit, he didn't look overjoyed. If anything, he looked worse than she felt at the moment.

He didn't respond to her comment. Instead, he leaned down, obviously searching for the sign-in sheet, which she'd just filed. "You still want me to sign him out, right?" he said, glancing up.

You didn't need Gypsy genes to know something was

wrong. Very wrong. "Mark, what's going on? Have you heard something about the arson investigation? Oh, my God, they're not charging you with that, are they? Did that witch try to cut a deal?"

He reached out and touched her arm, obviously trying to quell her growing anxiety. "No. Nothing's changed there. I was told our lab sent some residue to the state crime lab for analysis, but they still haven't gotten back the results. It's the holidays."

His casual attitude angered her. "What do you mean it's the holidays? So what? Don't the people who work in those places realize a person's life hangs in the balance?"

"Alex, the intensity of the fire means there weren't a lot of clues to sift through. Even if the lab reports come back negative—meaning there was no trace of an accelerant beyond the normal chemicals found in a meth lab, that doesn't mean there wasn't a bomb. In fact, it could mean whoever set the fire was either an extremely clever arsonist—or someone who was good at investigating arson fires."

Her stomach clenched in a way that brought back the nausea she'd been fighting most of the day.

"At this point, it's my word against a dead drug addict's," he said solemnly.

"A guy your ex-mother-in-law had killed."

"Supposedly."

"Why'd she do that? Just so she could use the gun to frame you for his murder?"

He sighed. "Her boyfriend said the guy was threatening to recant his statement. Partly because the D.A. wouldn't back off from his third-strike charges until he produced some kind of proof that I put a bomb in that house and partly because Odessa hadn't paid him the money she'd promised him." He threw up his hands. "These are people whose lives are centered on drugs—making, buying, selling, using. There's no way for someone who isn't part of that cycle to understand how they think."

"Okay. I get that. But you're not part of the cycle. So, why haven't they cleared you as a suspect?"

"Because Odessa is now the second person who claims I did it."

"Why would they believe her?"

Mark looked toward where his son was sitting with Luca and Gemilla. Maya had left half an hour earlier with Rob, but Gregor apparently was running late.

"She's given them some new information that supposedly speaks to motive."

"*Your* motive?"

He nodded.

"What is it?"

He blew out an impatient-sounding breath and shrugged. "I'd rather not say. They're running some tests. Nothing's going to come of it, but I don't want to talk about it until we get confirmation."

She could tell that this was a serious, potentially life-altering test. She knew about those. She had one sitting on the bathroom counter. She just hadn't decided whether or not to use it.

She'd bought the home pregnancy test kit months ago to have on hand when she started going through the in-vitro process. A bit prematurely, granted, but the gesture had made her feel as if the process was actually going to take place. All day long though, she'd been vacillating about whether or not to use it now. She wasn't pregnant. She couldn't be. But something weird was going on with her body.

"Okay," she said. "I didn't mean to pry. I just wanted you to know that most of the schools are doing a partial day on Friday. We're going to have a whole-school party in the afternoon, and Braden is welcome to come. You are, too, of course."

"A Christmas party?"

"A non-secular, all-inclusive, politically correct *holiday* party," she said trying to keep her tone light. His raised eyebrow told her she'd failed. "Okay, it's a Christmas party. We ask each child to bring a book—new or used, which we donate to battered women shelters." She added in a whisper, "I have new books to replace the old ones. My gift to my students."

He looked at her a moment then nodded. "He'll be here."

FIFTEEN MINUTES LATER, Mark and Braden were walking toward Mark's truck, which he'd parked in front of the Hippo, when a man came charging across the cul-de-sac.

Alex's cousin, Gregor, Mark realized once his initial police-trained reaction died down.

"Hey, you two, glad I caught you."

Mark wasn't sure what that meant, but he paused. "Pardon?"

"Luca has been asking if he could have Braden over to play. The poor kid doesn't have a lot of friends in the area and with my hours at work, I don't usually get home early enough to arrange anything. But, I'm taking a personal day tomorrow—have to run out to Montevista Hospital to check on MaryAnn, but I'll be back before the kids get home from school. I thought maybe Braden and Luca could play together at our house instead of going to the Hippo. We've got lots of toys. And video games. Age appropriate. Nothing violent."

Mark looked at his son. "Would you like to go to Luca's house tomorrow?"

Braden nodded vigorously. You didn't need to be a mind reader to see the hope and excitement in his son's face.

"Okay," Mark said. "Sounds good."

"Cool. Why don't you two come over for a minute right now—after I get my kids, of course, and make sure you really want to do this, Braden? The place isn't the neatest. Luca's mom has been away."

Mark didn't have any reason to hurry home. "Sure. Why not? Let's put your backpack in the truck, son."

The timing worked out perfectly. Gregor and his kids returned almost immediately. The two boys shot across the street without really looking for traffic, which, thankfully, was nonexistent.

"I'll be right there, Bray," Mark hollered after his son. To Gregor, he explained, "I'd better tell Alex not to expect him or she might call search and rescue. We had an incident last week with Braden's grandmother."

"Yeah, I heard. MaryAnn's mom is a pain in the butt, too, but fortunately she lives in Hawaii."

Gregor turned and, with his daughter at his side, followed the boys across the street. Gemilla was a pretty little girl who never seemed too animated unless Maya was around. Once she and her father reached the driveway of their home, she dashed inside ahead of Luca and Braden.

His son had a friend. The fact was almost enough to make Mark choke up. Friends were important. He'd never had too many until he'd been in high school. With a father like his, bringing a buddy home was asking for trouble.

He'd always assumed his son would have a different kind of life, but this was probably the first time anyone had asked Braden to come over and play. The thought made his chest hurt. He was a failure as a father. In so many ways he was losing count.

Taking a deep breath, he knocked on the pastel purple door of the Hippo. When Alex didn't answer, he tried the knob—and was surprised to find it open. "Alex," he called, walking inside.

She wasn't at her desk and the lights were off in the daycare area so he headed toward the hallway leading to her rooms. He called her name again but didn't want to disturb her if she was on the phone or something.

"Alex, it's me…Mark. Alex?"

He walked into her bedroom. Nobody was there. He started to leave, thinking she might have slipped out the side door and walked to her mother's when he heard a low moan followed by a voice crying, "Oh, my God. That's not possible."

He reversed course and charged into the brightly lit master bath. Alex was sitting on the edge of her oversize tub, holding a box in one hand and a plastic wand of some kind in the other. Between the look on her face—a mixture of disbelief and shock—and the overly large initials on the box that clearly stood for Early Pregnancy Test, Mark figured out what she was shaken up about.

Shock, hurt, fury—the combination of emotions hit so fast he could barely think, but one thought crowded out all the rest. "You lied to me."

She looked up. "Huh?"

"You said there wasn't anyone else."

The box slipped from her fingers, which had started to

shake. The color drained from her face, and Mark realized she was about to faint. He rushed to her side and carefully eased her head down between her knees. He felt her body trembling. She tried speaking but he couldn't make out what she was saying.

"Twice in one lifetime," he muttered. "How big a sucker am I? Not once, but twice. Were you going to try to palm this kid off on me, too?"

She reared back, her color greatly improved. "What are you talking about? Why are you yelling at me? Wait. Why are you here? Where's Braden?"

"I'm the one asking questions. What is this?" He wrenched the white plastic stick out of her fingers.

"It's none of your business."

"I understand that. You slept with some guy a month or two ago and suddenly figured out you were pregnant. But you told me there wasn't anyone else."

"There wasn't."

"We slept together a week ago. Don't tell me this thing works that fast. That kind of trick only works once."

She shook her head and grabbed the stick back. "I have no idea what you're talking about. I've been on the highest dose of birth control pills known to man for years. I stopped taking them a couple of months ago. I've had one period since then, and I was due to start yesterday. When that didn't happen…"

"You whipped out your handy-dandy pregnancy test? Who keeps those lying around?"

"Someone who wants to—who plans to—get pregnant."

"You planned this?"

She looked at the ceiling. "I didn't plan on sleeping with you. I had no idea you were going to be here last week.

I *planned* on using a donor from a sperm bank as soon as my doctor said I was ovulating and it was safe."

"What do you mean *safe?*"

"The cysts may return. Nobody knows for certain if I can get pregnant."

Mark glanced at the plastic indicator. "What does that say?"

She let out a sigh. "It's probably a false positive. There's no way we could have gotten pregnant from one time—okay, two, but still the same night. I mean, I know you said that's how it happened with Tracey, but I never really believed you."

"You didn't?"

She shook her head. "If this thing is right, then I was wrong."

He slumped forward, resting his elbows on his knees. "No, you weren't."

"Really?"

He hadn't expected her to sound so hurt. "I *really* only slept with her that one night. One time. Honest. What I meant was, that's not how she got pregnant."

"Huh?"

"Her mother told me last week that I'm not Braden's father. Tracey was sleeping with another guy. She knew she was pregnant when she and I…" He stopped short of using the only word that applied. "According to Odessa, Tracey set out to seduce me because she figured I'd feel so guilty I'd marry her."

"Why?" Alex cried. "Why not just marry the other guy?"

Mark could barely bring himself to repeat the horrible possibility that had been haunting him for a week. "He was a drug dealer, for one thing. He also had a bad temper and most people considered him dangerous. Why she slept with him in the first place is anybody's guess, but apparently she didn't want that kind of life for her kid."

"Oh." The compassion in her eyes made Mark feel like a jerk since he'd felt nothing but fury toward his ex-wife when Odessa had told him about Tracey's supposed plan to sucker him into marrying her.

Neither spoke for a minute, then Alex grabbed his arm. "Oh, no, don't tell me that man is still around. He's not going to try to get custody of Braden, is he?"

Mark shook his head. "No. He's dead. He died with Tracey. That day. In the fire."

She clapped her hand to her mouth as if she might be sick. Suddenly her eyes went wide with horror. "No. You didn't know. They don't think…please, tell me they don't think that was your motive. If they put you in jail, then Odessa…no…no…she really does have a claim on Braden, doesn't she?"

She started to cry, tears spilling down her cheeks, but she dashed them away with her hands and a second later stood up. She turned to face him, legs spread in a fighting stance. "No. She can't have him. I'll take him. Or…or one of my sisters if…if not me. She's a horrible, horrible person, Mark. She can't have that precious little boy. She'll destroy him."

He stood up, too, and crushed her, sobbing, to his chest. Such a kind heart. An honest heart. He should have known she'd never lie to him. She and Tracey were as different as good and evil.

Chapter Seventeen

Alex wasn't sure how long they stood there, Mark holding her, providing comfort and reassurance that all would be okay. She could almost believe it in his arms, but slowly the reality of the situation took over.

He had a son—a little boy who thought of Mark as his father. A little boy who needed Mark's entire focus. And she wasn't helping things.

She gently pushed away from him and walked to the vanity. Bending over, she splashed cool water on her face then used a towel that Mark handed her. "Feeling better?" he asked.

She nodded. "I think so. I've been on a bit of a hormone roller coaster today. Sorry I yelled at you."

"It's okay. You should have been there when I found out. Odessa was damn lucky there were three cops present."

"Do you believe her?"

He took a breath and let it out. "I don't know. Zeke ordered a DNA test. Just a swab on the inside of your cheek, but I don't give a damn what the results say. Braden is my son. Blood or not."

Alex knew she'd never loved Mark more. But that didn't

solve her problem. His first response to seeing her with the pregnancy kit had been to accuse her of cheating on him— and they weren't even dating.

"What do we do now?" he asked.

"Nothing."

She stood up and took a breath to clear the fuzzy dots from her vision. Her legs were as wobbly as heck, but she was entitled. Her world had turned upside down—a good reason for wobbly legs.

"Nothing?"

She wanted to crawl under the covers and hide, but that would only postpone the inevitable, and procrastination wasn't her style. "Okay. Let's talk. Just us. Now. Where's Braden?"

"At your cousin's. I came back to tell you he was going there tomorrow after school to play."

Luca and Braden's friendship was the one good thing to come out of all of this, she thought. "Let me call Gregor and see if he minds keeping Braden a little longer."

Minutes later, she and Mark sat down across from each other in her little TV nook. "Here's the deal. My body is kinda screwed up—partly from the operation, partly from the birth-control pills. The pamphlet that came with the test says the results may not be accurate this early. I might not know for sure for a month or two. And given the state of my reproductive organs, anything could happen in that time."

"A miscarriage?"

She nodded. "I'm in my mid-thirties, Mark. Nine years ago, this probably wouldn't have been an issue. But my body has been through a lot since then." She looked down and tenderly rubbed her belly. "Getting pregnant this soon after going off the pill…? That just doesn't happen. I honestly don't know what to believe."

"How do you feel?"

She wasn't sure how to answer. Living with the monthly pain that came from her cysts had made her acutely sensitive to changes inside her body. But since she'd never been pregnant, she didn't know if the symptoms she was experiencing were pregnancy-related or just premenstrual.

"Um…different. My breasts are tender. That used to happen when I got my period, but this time I haven't had continuous severe pain—only a little nausea. That's why I used the test."

"Did your doctor say there was any reason—physically—that you couldn't carry a baby to term?"

A baby. She couldn't—wouldn't—get her hopes up. "Not really, but he didn't seem very confident about my ability to conceive. He was worried about scar tissue blocking my fallopian tubes."

"What if you are pregnant?"

She shook her head. "I don't want to think about that right now."

"Why? Because of the fight we had?"

"No. Well, partly. I…love you, Mark. I always have, but that doesn't mean we're good for each other. Producing a baby together doesn't guarantee we'd be a happy family. Two children right off the bat? With our history? Sounds like a recipe for disaster."

He didn't argue with her, but he didn't look convinced, either.

"I promise to let you know as soon as I know something. I'll make an appointment to see my doctor right after the holidays. Why stress about what might happen if this is just a false alarm?"

Her fatalistic tone was so unlike the Alex he knew and loved, Mark wasn't sure how to react. She was right about one thing, though, this development was a lot to absorb, and until he knew for certain that he had a job—and wasn't going to prison for a crime he hadn't committed—he wasn't in a position to make promises he couldn't keep.

But he knew her. And he could picture her spending the rest of the night worrying and pacing and fretting, so acting on impulse, he said, "I'm taking Braden to buy a Christmas tree. Will you come with us?"

She shook her head. "No. I can't. Oh, heavens, I'm a mess. And I have a million things to do. Christmas is only five days away."

"And knowing you, you have every last detail taken care of. I've put off getting a tree because…well, frankly, I just can't get in the holiday spirit."

"Not surprising," she said wryly. "I'd probably be pretty grinchy myself if not for the thirty-plus kids in my care."

"Then maybe the two of us together could produce enough Christmas spirit to fool a little kid whose previous holiday experiences have been pretty shaky."

"What do you mean? Tracey didn't celebrate Christmas?"

"She did. I'm sure she tried to make special memories for him, but with her mother involved…"

"Say no more. I'll get my coat. Do you have decorations?"

"A few."

"Well, you've come to the right place, my friend—Christmas Central. If I don't have what you need, my mother does."

About forty minutes later they left Alex's with two giant boxes of Christmas decorations in the back of the truck. Braden was so excited he could barely sit still.

"T-tr-tree? A b-b-big one?"

The more excited he got, the more pronounced his stutter became, but Mark had learned not to correct him. For the most part, he understood what Braden was trying to say, so why draw attention to his problem—especially on a special night like this?

"Mom and I always get our trees from the Boy Scouts. The lot is a couple of miles down on Charleston Boulevard. Shall we try there first?"

"Sure. Why not?"

"J-jingle b-bells," Braden called out from the backseat.

Mark glanced at Alex, who leaned forward and turned up the volume on the radio. The kid certainly had acute hearing. Mark hadn't even realized there was music playing.

He found himself tapping his toe as Braden and Alex harmonized to a country-western version of "Jingle Bell Rock." His smile grew as he realized that this was exactly the kind of holiday memory he'd hoped to create for his son, but it wouldn't have been the same without Alex.

Just at that moment, she looked at him and touched his arm. With a quick look toward the backseat, she put one finger to her lips and pointed toward Braden. Mark cocked his head and listened.

"Jingle bell, jingle bell, jingle bell rock..." the little boy sang. Without stuttering.

"What the—" he exclaimed.

The singing stopped.

Alex shifted in her seat and said, "You sing really nicely, Braden. Good job." Then she quickly turned and pointed toward a cheerfully lit tree lot. "There it is. I hope they still have some good ones."

Mark wanted to ask her about his son's temporary cure, but he didn't get the chance. Moments later, Alex and Braden, hand in hand, disappeared into a forest of dark green spruce and pines. To Mark's surprise, the place was packed with shoppers. He'd figured he was the last person in town to buy his tree. Not so, apparently, but the stock was going fast. There was a long line at the checkout counter.

"Alex? Braden?" he called.

"We're over here," she answered.

He found them examining a shoulder-high, candle-shaped tree that looked healthy and smelled great. "This variety is my personal favorite, but I can never remember what it's called. White spruce?"

Mark found a tag, but the black scrawl only gave the price, not the kind. "Doesn't matter what it is. I like it. How 'bout you, Bray? Is this the tree for us?"

Braden nodded exuberantly.

"Okay, then." He rubbed his hands together and picked it up. The night was brisk, but the trees and the crowd of people made him feel as if he'd been transported to a forest with a festive group of revelers. Tinny carols from a boom box filled the air. The line moved with surprising speed, and soon they were headed home with their eighty-dollar tree.

One quick stop for take-out tacos and they were set.

"I appreciate your cousin giving me his old tree stand, but I can see why he got rid of it," Mark complained an hour later—from beneath the branches of his new tree. "It's a pain in the butt to adjust."

His house smelled of pine and burritos. He could see Alex's ankles and stocking feet since she was holding the tree upright. Giving his arm a rest from the awkward position required to tighten the oversize screws that braced the trunk, he laid his head on the carpet and tickled her toes.

"Stop. Braden. Come help your dad before I kick him," she said with a squeal. She hopped back slightly and leaned down enough to give him stern look. A preschool-teacher look that probably worked on a four-year-old but only made him want to kiss her.

Braden left his job of sorting ornaments and raced to Mark's side, dropping to his knees. "You hold this one, bud, while I crawl around to the other side. Without the right leverage," he said with a grunt of effort, "the darn thing doesn't want to turn."

Braden copied Mark's pose and used both hands to grip the silver screw. His top teeth were clamped down on his bottom lip in a study of concentration. Mark's heart did a crazy lift and fall. Braden was the spitting image of one of the few pictures Mark had from his own childhood. Tears clouded his eyes. He blinked furiously and focused on finishing the job.

"There," he said, crawling backward. "We did it."

Alex applauded. "Good job, both of you. Now, for the lights."

They followed Braden's lead—the more the better. Alex wisely plugged in every set before they looped them around the branches. Three of the hand-me-down strands didn't work. She tossed them into the garbage.

Next came the ornaments. Mark hadn't planned to bother with the box of Christmas stuff that had been Tracey's and was now stored in his closet. But then Alex asked, "Does Braden have any personalized ornaments? Like 'Baby's First Christmas' or anything?"

The cardboard box wasn't in great condition. The silver duct tape across the top was peeling in places. Mark ripped it off and pushed aside the flaps. Memories assaulted him. The entire top layer was made up of strands of tiny gold beads. Tracey had bought them their first year together. Braden had been too young to understand, but they'd still dressed him in red and white and propped him up near their small but festive tree. He'd accidentally grabbed the beads in his tiny fist, and Tracey had panicked, thinking he was going to choke on one.

There'd never been any question in Mark's mind that Tracey had loved their son. Unfortunately, some of her choices had put Braden at risk. Not intentionally, he knew. When she wasn't drinking or using drugs, Tracey had been a good mom.

"Ooh," Braden said. "P-pretty."

"Very classy," Alex said. "I like these."

While Braden and Alex made a game of draping the golden necklaces around the tree, Mark dug deeper. Most of the decorations he didn't recognize. He and Tracey had spent more holidays apart than they had together, but one item caught his interest. A small photo album.

"Hey, Bray, come take a look at this. Your mom kept pictures of you from every Christmas. Here you are as a little tiny baby. You loved lying on the floor looking at the lights on the tree. I remember how we used to put you in your car seat and drive around to see all the lights."

He looked at Alex and admitted, "I think the motion of the car put him to sleep, but Tracey and I enjoyed seeing the elaborate decorations. She always said she was going to have a big house with thousands of lights on it."

A deep sadness filled his soul. He'd hated his ex-wife at the end, but they'd shared tender moments of hope and possibilities, too. There was even a remote chance they might have made a go of things if Odessa hadn't shown up. At a gut level, Mark had understood the hold the woman had had on Tracey—similar to the hold his father had had on his mother. And, sadly, the results had been the same— Mark hadn't been able to save either of them.

Braden settled down in Mark's lap and turned a couple of pages. He paused and pointed to an image of two women—Tracey and someone Mark had never met—with Braden between them. Braden's finger was shaking slightly as he touched it to the plastic. "P-p-ig-g-eon."

The name seemed tougher than it should have been for him to say. His little brow was furrowed tightly, and Mark could feel his tension. Instinct told him the little boy was trying to impart something important.

Alex dropped to her knees beside them. "Can I see?"

Braden handed her the album.

"Your mom looks really happy in this picture. Were you having a party?"

He nodded.

"Is this lady a friend of hers?"

"Uh-huh," he grunted. "P-pi-geon."

"Like the bird?" She made a flapping motion.

He grinned and nodded.

"Hmm. That's an unusual name. I bet if she was a good friend of your mom's, she might be able to tell us some things about Tracey's life. Friends keep secrets for each other." She looked at Mark pointedly.

Nice, he mouthed over Braden's head.

Braden's yawn cut the evening short. Alex insisted on calling a cab to take her home so Mark could give Braden a bath and get him in bed on time.

He walked her to the door. "I don't know what this woman can tell us about Tracey's last days, but I'll check her out."

"Good," she said, putting on her gloves. She looked past him into the living room and smiled. "The tree looks great. The popcorn was an inspired idea. I bet someday when Braden is looking back, he'll remember how his father burned the first batch and we had to open all the windows to keep the smoke alarm from going off."

He leaned against the doorjamb. "Yeah, sure, rub it in. I never said I was a cook."

She leaned closer and patted his shoulder. "Don't feel bad. We always lose one batch at the preschool, too. It's a tradition."

He pulled her into his arms and kissed her. "Are you sure you won't stay?"

"I can't. I'll see you tomorrow—no, wait, Braden is going to Gregor's, but you're coming to the party on Friday, right?"

He nodded.

She smiled and kissed him again then dashed away as a horn sounded in the distance.

The party. He hadn't planned on attending, but something had changed tonight. Not just the fact she might or might not be pregnant. They'd deal with that when she found out for certain. No, what really clicked in his mind was the undeniable truth that they belonged together. They fit. She belonged with him and Braden.

As he walked toward the bathroom, mentally preparing for Braden's resistance to his bath, he realized that convincing Alex they had a future together wasn't going to be easy. But he was prepared to do whatever it took—once he was free of the lingering doubt about the cause behind Tracey's death.

Chapter Eighteen

It took Zeke two days to assemble a file on Pigeon, aka Patti Gionella. Two frustrating days for Mark.

Her name had turned up right away on a search through Metro files, but the woman had either moved away or disappeared beneath police radar since her last brush with the law. Her rap sheet included one charge of prostitution, a couple of drug-related busts and two domestic-disturbance complaints. The last incident had been one of Tracey's cases after she'd returned from maternity leave.

"Do you suppose this is how Tracey and Pigeon met?" Mark asked, looking over Zeke's shoulder at the file he had no business seeing. He was still relieved of duty and was supposed to be sitting around twiddling his thumbs.

"Seems likely, although look at the other name in this report," Zeke said, tapping his finger at the bottom of one page.

Mark read it and let out a soft whistle. "Small world, isn't it?" Years of experience, both as a cop and as an arson investigator, told him they'd stumbled across a good lead. This was too big a coincidence to ignore. His ex-wife's best friend had at one time been living with the drug dealer who'd died in the same fire as Tracey. The man Odessa claimed was Braden's father.

"So let's try to establish a time line," Zeke said. "According to Odessa, Tracey had something going with this guy when you two started as partners. He was a small-time pusher, and either she was screwing him in return for a little juice or her mother is full of crap. You say Tracey was clean when you were together."

"I never saw any sign that she was using. She drank too much, but we know a lot of cops who escape into a bottle after work."

Zeke didn't disagree. "Since we don't have the DNA results back yet, we only have Odessa's word that Tracey and this bastard were sleeping together. What we do know for certain is the guy got popped for trafficking and was sent to Jean where he served three of six. He comes back to Vegas and hooks up with Pigeon long enough to knock her around. Tracey takes the call. He gets a slap on the hand. Since you and Tracey aren't together at this point, Tracey offers the girl a place to stay. Sound about right to you?"

Mark nodded.

"Until Odessa shows up some time after this holiday picture," Zeke said, pointing to the photo Mark had brought from home.

"That was always Odessa's MO. She'd drop in without warning and expect Tracey to take her in. I think it's safe to assume that once Odessa moved in, Pigeon split."

"When I asked Odessa, she said Pigeon went back to the lowlife scum who abused her in the first place, but then there's this." He held up an official-looking fax. "One Patricia Gionella participated in an out-patient rehab program a full three months before the meth lab went boom. The same program you said Tracey claimed to be participating in."

"Knowing Tracey, she kept in touch with Pigeon and provided an out when Pigeon needed help," Mark said. "For all her faults, Tracey had a good heart."

Zeke didn't appear convinced. "Or Tracey and Pigeon could have been partying together."

Mark threw up his hands. "That could be, too. I honestly don't know. By that point, Tracey and I were barely speaking. And when we did talk, we fought over Braden."

Neither spoke for a moment, then Zeke said, "One given is the fact that Tracey knows this jerk. If she had business with him—drugs or otherwise—would she have gone to a meeting unarmed?"

"Not the Tracey I knew."

Mark could see a number of scenarios unfolding the day Tracey had died. He'd assumed she'd been at the meth lab to buy drugs, but maybe there'd been another reason for her presence there. If she'd taken along a gun, anything could have happened, including an explosion.

"We have to locate this woman. She may have a bird name, but I'd bet my badge she didn't fly the coop," Zeke said.

Mark groaned. "You keep that up, and Santa is going to whiz right past your house Sunday night."

Zeke chuckled but didn't look apologetic about his failed wittiness. "Speaking of Santa, I heard you and Alex did a little decorating the other night."

"Bought a tree and put up lights. I burned the popcorn, but Alex and Braden still managed to string a few strands. That's when I found this album."

"Alex's mother is worried about her."

So am I. They'd talked on the phone, but she hadn't been home when he'd dropped by on his way to pick up Braden after the play date at Gregor's.

"Isn't Yetta going to be at the party this afternoon?"

Zeke nodded. "Yetta, Grace, Kate...the whole clan by the sound of it."

"Grace is in town?"

"She and Nick arrive at eleven. Have you met him? He's a decent guy. Got a good head on his shoulders. Applied for a captain's position in Detroit—well, some suburb, but same thing. According to Yetta, he was just told he didn't get the job. It went to some guy with DEA experience. They've got their own kind of drug problems."

"Hmm, too bad. Maybe he should move here and take your job." Mark laughed. "Oh, right, I forgot. You're never going to retire."

Zeke scowled and stood up. "Let's go find your little bird."

ALEX WIPED A BEAD OF SWEAT from her brow. The noise level was surely going to take the roof off, she thought. *Or the top of my head at the very least.*

"Hey, sis, are you okay? You don't look too hot," Liz said, pausing as she circulated with a pitcher of punch. She'd volunteered to refill cups to minimize the line at the refreshment table.

The Dancing Hippo holiday party had grown into such a popular affair Alex was afraid she might have to start limiting the invited guests to immediate family only. Currently, grandparents, friends and extended family were welcome to attend. And they did—en masse. Too mass-ive, she decided.

But, a part of her was loath to restrict what was for

many of her students a very important part of their holiday experience.

"No, I'm fine," Alex said, putting some starch in her spine. She wasn't feeling well, but nausea was a part of pregnancy, right? She hadn't confirmed her condition with another test, but her cramps had disappeared without her period showing up. And this morning she'd spent a good hour vomiting. A bad hour, actually. An hour she couldn't spare. "Is Grace here, yet?"

"Haven't seen her. You know she's always late. Maybe you should start the program."

"Good idea." Alex walked to the small raised platform where her students would be performing their songs and picked up one set of sleigh bells. She gave the leather strap with three brass orbs attached to it a shake. "Hello…Merry Christmas…Can I have your attention?"

Slowly the noise died down and people turned to face her.

"Welcome, everyone, to the Dancing Hippo's holiday party. I see some new faces this year, so let me introduce my staff." She called out the name of each of her aides. "Believe me, these dedicated ladies are the backbone of this enterprise, and your children are lucky to have them in their lives."

After a round of applause, she motioned for her sisters and her mother to step forward. "The Dancing Hippo has always been my personal dream, but it wouldn't have materialized without the support of my family. My mother, Yetta. My sisters, Liz, Kate and…" She scanned the audience.

As if on cue, the door opened and a woman in a faux-fur coat rushed in. "Grace," Alex exclaimed. "Straight from Detroit."

"Sorry I'm late," Grace said, squeezing through the

crowd to reach Alex. "The plane. The ice. Oh, you don't want to know."

The crowd laughed.

Alex was so happy to see her baby sister, she felt a little overwhelmed, but she managed to stifle her emotions. She cleared her throat and announced, "To start off our program, we're going to give you 'Jingle Bells' rap. Those of you with hearing aids are welcome to turn them down."

Liz helped pass out bells and arrange the students in order of height. The taller boys, William, Braden and Luca, would have been grouped together in the back, but William was missing. Alex frowned. Roberta was so good about letting Alex know if the family was scheduled to go out of town. She hoped everything was okay.

"Wait," she said softly when one eager bell ringer started shaking too soon. "All together now. Nice and loud. And don't forget to sing."

"Jingle bell, jingle bell, jingle bell *rap*," they sang. Of course, the last word was a shout, but delivered enthusiastically by the three- and four-year-olds. Under the cacophony of chimes, Alex swore she could hear Braden's voice. Clear and unbroken. Tears clouded her eyes, but she blinked them away.

Not in time to avoid getting caught by Grace. Her sister was staring at her as if Alex had a flashing sign over her head: Alert. Alert. Possibly Pregnant.

And, of course, once the performance was completed, Grace worked her way through the crowd to say, "Alexandra, we need to talk."

"You sounded just like Mom there." Alex pushed a platter of cookies—each decorated by her students, which

meant in some cases there was more frosting than cookie—
into her sister's hands. "Go. Mingle. I'm busy."

"But—"

"Later, Grace. You and Nick are here till the third of
January, right? We'll have plenty of time to talk."

"But—"

"Not now, Grace." ·

Her words seemed to carry above the hum of the crowd
and everyone turned to look at her. Alex was certain her face
was as red as the plush Santa hat on her head. "Be sure to take
each of the paintings that your child did home with you," she
called, making a sweeping gesture with her hand. "These are
real treasures that you'll want to keep to show your children's
children. Just ask my mom. Our four handprints are the first
decorations she hangs up every year. Isn't that right, Mom?"

Yetta was standing close enough for Alex to reach for
her hand and draw her onto the stage for a hug. A smatter-
ing of applause made her mother beam. "You've outdone
yourself today, dear. It's a lovely party."

"I need a bigger house."

"My mother used to say, 'It's not the size of the house,
it's the size of the heart.'"

Alex made a little "oh" sound. "I never heard that one,
but I like it. And thanks for your help, Mom. I really
couldn't have done this without you."

They hugged again—and were soon joined by Grace.
"Me, too. I need my Rom fix."

"Your husband-to-be is half Romani," Alex reminded her.

"Doesn't count. He's not a girl."

"I would hope not," Yetta said primly. "He's far too
handsome to be a woman."

"Speaking of handsome," Grace said, looking over Alex's

shoulder. "Is that major hunk who I think it is? Oh, my. No wonder you two are an item again. Way to go, Alex."

Alex groaned and spun on one heel. Her equilibrium spun, too, but her sister was there to steady her. Grace's perfectly plucked left eyebrow lifted the way a movie detective's might. Another clue. Damn.

Before Grace could say anything, though, the handsome hunk in question walked up to them. "Hi. Sorry I'm late. Zeke and I were…on a hunt."

Pigeon, Alex thought.

To Grace, he said, "Hello, Grace. Long time no see. I hear congratulations are in order."

Grace shook his hand. "Thank you. The same to you, right?"

Mark looked at Alex sharply.

Gulping, she hastily explained, "She means about Braden, don't you, Grace?"

Grace's lips formed a thoughtful moue as she looked from Mark to Alex and back again. "Of course. What else? You don't have news about the arson case, yet, do you?"

"Yet?" Alex asked.

"Zeke and Nikolai were on the phone the minute we landed. I swear they're closer friends than any of the guys Nick has introduced me to in Detroit. They speak the same language. Do you speak cop, too?"

Mark smiled. "Firefighter. Slightly different dialect. But if they speak slowly I can usually understand them."

Grace roared and gave Mark a quick hug. "I like you. There was a time I didn't, but now I do. See you later." She dashed off into the crowd.

Mark looked a little shell-shocked. "Wow. She's…"

"A presence. I know. But we love her." Clearing her throat,

which suddenly felt terribly parched and burning, Alex said, "I'm glad you're here, but what's the story with Pigeon?"

"We'll find her. Just a matter of time. I hate to ask, but could you keep Braden this afternoon? Zeke found out that Pigeon's mother and stepdad have a place in Indian Springs. We'd like to run up there and ask a few questions."

Alex was exhausted, utterly drained, but she couldn't say no. She knew how important this was to him, to Braden. "Sure," she said. "Kate planned to hang out at Mom's to visit with Grace, so I'm sure Maya and Braden will have a great time together."

And with any luck, I can grab a nap.

Chapter Nineteen

Mark left the Day Care with mixed emotions. Mostly, he felt guilty about asking Alex to keep Braden. She'd looked so tired. Beautiful, of course. The jaunty tilt of the plush red hat with the white trim fur almost matched her rosy cheeks.

Parking was at a premium today, with all the families of both the morning and afternoon classes attending the festivities, so Mark had to search for Zeke's car. He'd taken a few minutes to follow Braden on a guided tour of his art projects. More examples than Mark had expected to find since Braden only attended the school a couple of hours a day.

Braden had also presented Mark with a decorated box— the kind Mark had folded and assembled when he'd been a volunteer helping at the school.

"M-my h-hand," Braden had said, proudly.

"That's great, son. We'll hang it on the wall when we get home. This is the best gift ever." And he'd meant it. Mark was finally starting to feel as if things were going to work out—for him and for Braden.

He had to jog halfway around the block to find the unmarked Ford. To his shock, a stranger was sitting in the passenger seat.

The window rolled down. Zeke leaned over and said to Mark, "Nick Lightner, meet Mark Gaylord. Nick's coming with us. Since this is just an informal social call and all," he added, reminding both men of Mark's unofficial status where this investigation was concerned.

"The more the merrier," Mark said, getting into the backseat. He knew the only reason he was here was because of Zeke's friendship and determination to clear Mark's name.

"Sorry to butt in," the well-built man with wavy blond hair said. He looked more like a movie star than a cop. And he was half Romani? Mark wasn't sure he believed it.

"No problem, but aren't you supposed to be at the party? I saw your fiancée there."

The man ran a hand through his hair in a nervous mannerism. "Yeah, but all those kids? No, thanks. Zeke offered me a chance to go hunting, and I jumped onboard. Grace will understand."

"You got something against kids?" Mark asked.

Nick turned so Mark could see his face. "Not really. But, they're short and loud and…" His gaze dropped. "They scare the you-know-what out of me."

Mark would have laughed, but he could tell the man was serious. Big, strong cop unnerved by a group of preschoolers. He loved it.

"Well, that'll change when you have your own. I guarantee it. Grace strikes me as the equal-parent kind of woman. You'll be changing your share of diapers and doing your part when it's time for preschool."

Nick let out a long groan and slumped down in the seat. "Yep, I suspect you're right."

"Speaking of suspects…" Zeke said, yukking at his little joke. "Do we have an address for Pigeon's parents?"

"Mother," Mark clarified. "The dad is dead, according to her records. There was a stepdad, but I'm not sure he's living there now. The street number is on top of the folder. My notes are inside, if you want to take a look, Lightner."

Nobody spoke for a few miles while the newcomer read. "Hell," Nick said twenty minutes later. "They suspended you for this? A plea bargain with a three-strike loser? The man was a flake. It says here they're not even sure he was in town at the time of the fire. How would he know anything?"

Mark shrugged. "Supposedly, I have a motive and the expertise."

Nikolai snorted skeptically. He turned the page and read further until he startled visibly and looked at Zeke. "It says here that the dealer who died in the fire was known to have supplied Charles Harmon's sister with drugs."

Zeke glanced at Mark. "Really? I don't remember reading that."

Mark sat forward. "I pulled it off some report. Didn't figure it meant anything since Harmon's in jail, but his name always raises a red flag with me, considering his ties to the Rom community." He looked at Nick. "You're the guy who nailed him, right?"

Nikolai turned so he could see both Mark and Zeke. "With a little help from Grace," he said with a chuckle. "But the first call I got from Yetta came in late January. Harmon was on the street for a couple of months after that. I didn't even come to Vegas until the middle of February."

Zeke nodded. "That's true."

"What's your point? Harmon's sister has been dead for

years. Why would he wait so long to do something to the guy who sold her drugs?"

Nick shook his head. "I don't know, but I remember him bragging that the people who supplied her with drugs would be afraid to make him mad. I didn't pursue it because I was undercover at the time, but I definitely got the impression he had something to do with drug traffic in this area."

"Not surprising," Zeke said. "The guy thought he could build his own little syndicate of corruption without law enforcement giving a damn." Glancing at Mark in the rear-view mirror, he added, "I swear Harmon and your ex-mother-in-law would get along great. They both see the world only as it applies to them."

Mark agreed.

To Nick, Zeke said, "I think we could use some fresh eyes on this case. Want to do a little moonlighting while you're here?"

"My future wife would kill me."

"I might be able to make it worth your while—and toss in a little bonus that even Grace would like."

Mark heard an odd waver in Zeke's voice. He hunched closer, elbows on knees.

"Really?" Nikolai said, glancing at Mark. "What would that be?"

"My job."

"I ALWAYS FEEL LIKE GULLIVER when I sit at one of these tables," Grace said, yanking her short skirt down modestly.

Kate, who was partially hidden behind a tower of art papers topped by a gold foil-wrapped box and a chain of green and red construction-paper loops, plopped one elbow on the table and sighed. "What was the name of the place that he landed in?"

"I can't remember," Grace said. "But I bet Alex knows."

"Lilliput. The people were Lilliputians. They buried their dead heads downward because they believed that when redemption came, the earth, which was flat, of course, was going to flip over and they'd be restored, feet flat on the ground."

Alex noticed her sisters staring at her, mouths agape.

"I read Jonathan Swift. Don't look at me like that."

"Something's up with her," Grace said to Kate.

"Well, duh, you don't have to be a Gypsy psychic to know that," Kate returned, tossing a stray kernel of popcorn across the table. "Mom thinks she's in love."

"Mom thinks *Alex* is in love?"

"Of course, who did you think I meant?"

"Mom."

"That's what I said, Mom thinks she's—"

Alex let out a low gurgle and dropped her head to the table. "Stop it. You two are like a bad version of 'Who's on First?'"

"We're not talkin' baseball here," Grace said, but the twinkle in her eye told Alex she was joking.

"Or Abbott and Costello," Kate put in. "Mom might be in love, too, but she's not our concern at the moment. You are."

The smooth, cool tabletop brought instant relief to Alex's hot cheeks and forehead. "Why me?"

"Uh-oh. She's mumbling."

"I think she has a fever. Maya gets the same glassy look in her eyes when she's sick."

Sick? Like the flu?

A sudden thought hit her and she sat upright and

looked around. "Did anyone check my phone messages this morning?"

"I did," another voice called. "Mom told me to." Liz finished boxing up the donated books that she'd volunteered to deliver to the shelter on her way home and walked across the room to join her sisters. "Because you were so busy greeting people."

"Well, what were the messages?"

"There was just one. From Roberta. She said William was sick. He came down with the flu last night, and she'd try to pick up his artwork on Monday unless she caught it, too."

"The flu," Alex croaked. "I have the flu."

Grace made a face. "That's the first time I've ever heard anyone sound happy about being sick."

Alex looked around and realized all three of her sisters were staring at her. She swallowed. The burning pain in her throat made sense, now. It wasn't from throwing up. How could she have been so stupid?

"I thought I had morning sickness," she admitted.

Their collective gasp could have sucked the air out of a dozen balloons.

Before any of them recovered, she held up her hand. "I don't want to talk about it. When I'm feeling better, I will open my private life to your sisterly scrutiny…because I know you'll drive me mad until you know everything. But not now. I'm too wiped out. Remember what happened the last time I had the flu?"

Kate and Grace looked at each other and nodded. "You wound up in the hospital," Kate said.

"Because you always take care of yourself last," Grace added. "Go to bed, now."

"And drink lots of liquids," Liz added. She jumped to her feet and started toward the kitchen. "I'll brew you some tea."

"What about Braden?" Kate asked. "Can we take him to Mom's with us?"

Alex leaned forward and braced her hands on the tiny table. "He could stay here and watch a movie, but I don't want to expose him to any more of my germs. I feel terrible that I was breathing on those poor people today. They'll probably all be sick on Christmas."

Grace stood up, too. "Cut yourself a little slack, Typhoid Alex. It's winter, and you work in a germ factory. Where do you think you got the bug?"

"And remember what Mom always says, 'It's not the seed, it's the garden.' Or something like that," Kate put in before anyone could correct her. "You were probably more susceptible to the virus because this is such a hectic time for you, and you let yourself get run-down."

Alex couldn't argue with that logic—even if she'd had the energy.

Grace bent down to pat Alex's back. "Kate's right. I know how hard you push yourself to make the holidays special for your students. But look at you, Alex. You're white as Santa's beard. Now, go to bed and get some rest. I'll put a note on your door so Mark won't disturb you when he shows up for his kid. Okay?"

Kate put her warm hand over Alex's icy one. "Braden will be fine. He seems to adore Maya, and she's very protective of him. She told me the other day that she's decided to 'fix' his speech problem because she doesn't like the way the other kids look at him when he stutters."

Alex attempted a smile. If anyone could bring Braden

out of his shell and help him with his speech impediment, it was Maya.

As she shuffled down the hall, one hand on the wall to keep her balance, she heard the low murmurings of her three sisters. They were talking about her, of course. And her revelation that she'd had sex with Mark. No doubt they'd come to the same conclusion: their eldest sister was out of her mind.

Chapter Twenty

The address Mark had scribbled in his notes belonged to a 1970s-era Fleetwood mobile home, faded green with a curved bay window on the end facing the street. Three cats watched from their vantage point behind the glass as Mark, Zeke and Nikolai approached.

A small, slightly lopsided porch had been attached to the front door. Several strands of tiny white Christmas lights zigzagged from post to post. The cheap artificial turf underfoot was frayed and sun-bleached, but a fresh pine wreath adorned with shiny red balls hung beside the door.

Mark knocked.

"Coming…" a voice called.

A face appeared behind the glass storm door. A woman. Shoulder-length dishwater-blond hair. Extremely thin. Mark recognized her from the photograph.

"You're Pigeon. I'm Mark Gaylord. You knew my ex-wife."

Her pretty blue eyes went wide and round. She was probably in her mid-thirties, but the years hadn't been kind to her.

"Can we come in and talk to you for a few minutes?"

"Am I in trouble? My mom said I couldn't stay if I brought trouble with me."

Mark felt sorry for her, but he said, "These gentlemen are police officers, but they're not here to arrest you. They're investigating Tracey's death, and they were hoping to get some sense of what Tracey's life was like at the end. We thought you might be able to help us."

After a few moments of indecision, she opened the door and led them into the shabby but neat living room. The cats were now grouped together like a three-headed beast. "I have to go to work in half an hour. I'm a waitress. Don't make squat in tips, but I'm not quite ready to give Vegas another try. Bad things happen when I'm there."

"What kind of bad things?" Zeke asked, taking a seat on the sofa. "Drugs?"

"Uh-huh. Mom says I have codependent tendencies. Whatever that means. And I ran with the wrong crowd. In school and stuff."

"Did you know Amy Harmon when you lived in Vegas?" Nick asked. "She had a brother. Quite a bit older. He used to be a lawyer in town."

Her shoulders lifted and fell. "Name sorta rings a bell, but I don't really remember."

Mark withdrew the photograph he'd brought with him. "How did you and Tracey get to know each other, Pigeon?"

The woman laughed nervously and looked over her shoulder as if expecting someone to scold her. "Um, I don't go by that name anymore. That was my...um...street name, if you get my drift. Call me Patti. That was what Tracey called me. She said I wasn't anybody's bird."

Mark waited for her to go on.

"She was one of the cops that came to the house when

me and my old man were fighting. That was the second time we met. The first was when she busted me for soliciting. But I wasn't really. I was just trying to score some glass—" Mark and Nick exchanged a look that said they recognized one of the many street names for meth. "And somebody said this guy in a Mercedes would trade the stuff for a blow job. Seemed like a good deal at the time," she said with a self-conscious laugh. "Tracey let me go. She said the buyer in the car was as much to blame as me." Her smile seemed reflective—and sad.

"I was pretty bad off when your wife…um, I mean ex-wife, came to the house. I was bleeding all over everything from this cut above my eye." She pointed to a small silver scar that bisected her left brow. "She called the EMTs and followed me to the emergency room. When we talked I felt like she really understood what I was going through."

She let out a weighty sigh. "Trace got me in a program. It helped for a while. I was doing good. She said I could live with her as long as I was clean. That's when we took this picture," she said, smiling at the memory. "But then the doctor who was running the program got caught bonking his nurse or something. The place closed down and I…I…"

"You started using again?"

She nodded. "I fell back in with my old crowd, but things weren't good. I sorta freaked out, and I went to Tracey for help, but she wasn't doing so good herself. This was after she got hurt at work. Her mother had moved in and…" She shuddered in a way that told Mark a lot. "The pain pills she was taking for her back made her kinda loopy and depressed. I think it really bummed her out when she lost her job."

Patti looked at Zeke and frowned. "That wasn't right, you know. She was a good person, and she did good when she was a cop. You guys hung her out to dry just because she made one mistake and lost her temper."

Zeke appeared to agree with her. "Unfortunately, she beat up a suspect, and somebody with a movie camera caught it on tape. The department didn't have a lot of choice in the matter."

"Well, she deserved better," Patti said, showing surprising spirit. "But Trace did have a temper. Her mom was the same way. And when those two started fighting, me and Braden would run and hide."

She looked at Mark. "I heard you got custody of him. Tracey wouldn't have wanted Odessa to be raising him. Sometimes, I thought she hated her mother worse than she hated Tom-Tom."

"Who?"

She looked at her hands, which were clenched so tightly Mark could see her knuckles white against her skin. "My ex. Tracey and Odessa knew him, too."

Mark's stomach clenched. "Odessa told me that Tracey and this Tom guy were an item before Trace and I got married. Is that true?"

Patti shrugged. "Don't know. Tracey hated him. That was for sure. When she found out I was getting my stuff from him, she went ballistic. Grabbed her gun, sent Braden to the neighbor lady next door and drove me straight to his place."

At the mention of the word *gun,* Mark looked at Zeke, who asked, "Do you know what kind of gun?"

She shook her head. "I was pretty messed up at the time. All I remember is her yelling at me and saying something about putting an end to the poison. She drove my car 'cause hers was low on gas. When we got there, she made me wait in the car."

Mark couldn't see her face because her chin was practically buried in the throat of her waitress uniform. "What happened?"

"She didn't come out for a long time. I got scared and I started to go after her in case Tom-Tom done something to her, you know?" She looked up. Tears filled her eyes, threatening to spill down her cheeks at any moment. "I only made it a few steps when there was a big explosion. I didn't really see what happened because the force threw me backwards and I covered up my head to keep from getting hit with boards and glass and stuff."

Mark could picture the image all too clearly, and, as always, he felt sick to his stomach thinking about Tracey inside the inferno that followed the explosion. Investigators had recovered two bodies burned beyond recognition. Dental charts had been needed to ID both of them. One was Tracey. The other, a man named Thomas Johns, with two dozen aliases. The guy's rap sheet started when he was twelve.

"So, Tracey's decision to visit this meth lab was impromptu…er, spur of the moment?" Nick asked. "Nobody else knew you were going to be there that day?"

She shook her head.

"And Tracey wasn't a regular there? She wasn't buying from this Tom-Tom guy?" Zeke questioned.

Her backbone stiffened. "Tracey was off that shit completely. She only went there to make that a-hole pusher stop cooking the crap. She said she was giving him a warning— to leave Vegas or she'd turn him in."

Mark almost smiled. That sounded like his ex-wife.

Willful, independent and cocky at the wrong moments. They'd butted heads more than once in the short time they'd been partners, and their inability to communicate had played hell on their marriage.

"Thank you, Pi…Patti. I wish we'd talked to you sooner."

She stood up when the men did. "You probably wouldn't have been able to. I was so shook up by what happened, I went underground. Came pretty damn close to dying. That's when I reached out to my mom for help. She'd just broken up with Ed, her second husband, and moved to this place. Mom said I could stay as long as none of my past followed me up here. You're not gonna make me go back, are you?"

Mark looked at Zeke. He couldn't see any reason they couldn't close the case. The woman had no reason to lie, and her version of the story proved that Mark couldn't possibly have known when Tracey was going to be at the drug house. Mark was no longer a suspect in her death.

"No, ma'am. You've helped us a great deal and we appreciate your cooperation. You and your mother have a happy Christmas."

Mark lingered on the little porch a moment longer after she showed them out. Once Zeke and Nick were out of earshot, he said, "Patti, Odessa told me something a few days ago. I don't want to believe her, but maybe you know the truth. Is there any chance that dealer, Tom-Tom, is Braden's real dad?"

Her expression looked torn. "I wish I could tell you no, but I honestly don't know. Tracey hated the guy but she never really said why. They might have had some kind of thing going in the past, but I don't know what. I'm sorry."

Mark was, too. In a fairy tale, she'd have solved all his problems and he could return to Las Vegas to live happily ever after. But his life had never been that simple. "No problem. I just thought I'd ask since you two were close."

He trudged down the steps, but stopped when she said, "What I do know is Braden used to cry at night and ask for his daddy. Poor little kid. Seemed pretty normal till his grandma moved in. Then he started having terrible nightmares, but I didn't blame him. Odessa was enough to scare anybody. I'm sure lucky my mom isn't like that. Tracey did pretty good for herself, considering…"

Her words stayed with him all the way back to Vegas.

ALEX AWOKE TO COMPLETE darkness. At least, she thought she was awake. She might have been dreaming. A fever dream. Her sheets were soaked from sweat, but she felt too weak to get up and change them. Instead, she rolled to the other side of her bed and pulled the pillow over her head.

The pillowcase smelled like Mark.

Another dream, she thought. She'd changed the bedding since their night together. Hadn't she?

"I'm losing it," she muttered, squeezing her eyes tight.

"Not my princess."

The words echoed in her mind. The voice was so dear to her she almost started to cry. Dad. She hadn't heard him speak that clearly and succinctly since his stroke.

"Oh, Daddy, I miss you."

"But I'm right here, honey. I never left. Not really."

Alex's eyes flew open and she lifted her head. Her louvered blinds were closed, but tiny horizontal beams of light cast a strange, striped pattern on the wall opposite the windows. And there, in a zebra-like silhouette, was the image of her father as she remembered him best. Not so tall, but big. *Larger than life* was how his obituary had described him.

Hands in his pockets. Top three buttons of his neatly pressed shirt open, with a white undershirt showing at the throat.

She sat up. "Dad?"

The cool air made gooseflesh stand up on her arms and she drew the down comforter to her chest.

The apparition never wavered, although his hands did make a jiggling motion in his pockets, and Alex swore she could hear the dull tinkle of silver dollars. Music to the ears of the four little girls who had clambered for his attention. "Me, Daddy. Me, Daddy. I wanna buy some candy." Or dolls. Or tapes. Or clothes. Or lipstick.

The last, she knew, had really made him sad. His little Gypsy princesses were growing up, and he was bound to lose each one to some man. A man who offered more than silver coins. Even the Gypsy King couldn't compete with love, companionship, children and family.

Alex had been certain that Mark was her guy. Her soul mate. Even her mother had backed Alex's choice— much to her husband's horror. Alex had overheard them arguing one night.

"Mark is a good person. His soul is strong and honest and filled with light. Why are you so against him?" Yetta had asked.

"Because he can't keep up with her. He lets her call the shots, and that's going to backfire some day. He'll disappoint her. I know he will," her father had replied.

"How did you know, Dad? How did you know that Mark would eventually let me down?"

The jingling stopped. "Because he reminded me of myself."

The cryptic answer baffled her. "But you're...you

were...the best man I ever knew. You would never cheat on Mom."

"There's more than one way to hurt the ones you love."

The bribe he took with Charles. Alex had heard the whole sad tale months earlier.

"Dad, what happened then was business. You were just trying to take care of us—the way you always took care of everybody and kept this family together."

His soft laugh was one she knew well. "That's your mother you're describing. When Yetta and I first met, I didn't have two of these to rub together." He held up a pair of silver dollars to the light. "She put down roots and grew a family. She let me take credit for everything, but think about it, Alexandra. Your sisters knew who to turn to for help. You are the only one who trusted me to solve her problems."

He had a point. Although Alex felt close to her mother, she'd generally sought out Ernst's help on the myriad dilemmas of life: boys, dating, cars, career choices. Ernst had seemed to understand her better.

"Because you and I are more alike, Dad."

"Bossy?"

She'd been called that. "Am I?"

"You're a teacher, Alex. But sometimes even the best student fails the test."

"What do you mean?"

She looked at the shadows for an answer, but the specter was gone. The lines of light were just lines of light. The jingling sound was just the breeze dancing through the wind chime on her patio.

Her tears returned and she plopped down, hugging her pillow to her chest. "Dad..." she sobbed. "Come back. I need you. I need to know what to do. I trusted Mark once, and he let me down. Just like you said he would. Now what do I do?" The last came out as a hysterical wail that seemed to echo off the walls of her bedroom.

A moment later, a new form—large and very real—came charging into the room. "Alex? What's wrong? Are you okay?"

She let out a gasp and scrambled backward against the headboard, certain she'd lost her mind. First, a ghost, then Mark. "Wh-what are you doing here?"

"Braden and I are sleeping in your guest room."

"Why?"

"Because your mother said you were sick—real sick—and the last time that happened you wound up in the ER. She wanted someone over here, and I volunteered."

Her adrenaline rush left her and she sank down on the mattress, pulling the covers over her head. "I'm contagious. Go away. I'm gonna live. Unfortunately."

His chuckle sounded closer. "Well, as long as you're awake, drink some of this stuff your sister sent over. Something to help your stomach and balance your electrolytes. She said it would be good for your condition."

Suddenly furious—certain her siblings had been talking about her behind her back, she sat up. "I hate my sisters."

"Well, they love you. They called all the parents who were here today to warn them about the flu bug making its rounds."

"They did?"

"Uh-huh." He turned on the bedside lamp. It wasn't terribly bright but it still took Alex a few seconds to see clearly. When she did, she had to swallow twice to regain her composure. Mark without a shirt. Calendar material. "You must be cold." His nipples were puckered.

He chafed his arms. "Yeah, I gotta do laundry. No

undershirts. But I'm fine. Let me see you drink that whole glassful. I set it there when I checked on you. You were dead to the world, I might add."

Was that before or after I had a conversation with my father? she wondered.

She took the glass, which appeared to be cloudy apple juice, and took a drink. The taste was *not* apple juice. "Yuck. What is this?"

"Liz told me the name, but I can't remember. She's going to start selling it."

Alex stuck out her tongue. "To whom? People without taste buds?"

His low chuckle seemed filled with humor. Something was different about him. But instead of asking, she downed the rest of her vinegar-flavored drink, then handed Mark the glass. "She's not a doctor, you know."

"But she is pushy."

"Yeah, a family trait."

He turned to leave. "You'd better go back to sleep."

"Wait. I want to ask you something. Would we have made it—as a couple—if what happened between you and Tracey hadn't happened?"

Mark turned around with a thoughtful frown on his face. He sat down on the end of the bed and looked at the glass in his hand. "I don't know, Alex. We were moving forward so fast—we met, moved in together, got engaged—all in under a year. You started talking about having babies right away...." He looked up. "I'm not saying that was a bad thing, but I remember feeling a little nervous. Like I'd stepped into a river and the current was taking me downstream faster than I could swim. Do you know what I mean?"

She did.

"My father told me you had more growing up to do, but I wouldn't listen."

"He did? I know he never liked me, but I never really understood why."

"I think you two were too much alike."

"Really? I wish that were true. He was a good man."

So are you. "When we were together, did I ever treat you like one of my students?"

His brows wriggled luridly. "Maybe in my fantasies."

She laughed. "You seem different tonight. Did something happen?"

He nodded. "Yeah. Something good. I'll tell you all about it tomorrow." He stood up then walked over to her and placed a tender kiss on her brow. "Go to sleep, princess. Life will look brighter in the morning."

A shiver passed through her. That was exactly what her father used to say when she had a bad dream.

Chapter Twenty-One

By Christmas eve, three days later, Alex was starting to feel human again. Both Saturday and Sunday had been marathon sleep sessions sprinkled with tender, well-intentioned nursing from her very worried family. Fortunately, there weren't any more visits from nocturnal ghosts.

Nor had Mark returned. She almost afraid to ask why. Either he or Braden had contracted her bug or he'd decided she was too high maintenance to bother with and had decided to stay as far away from her as possible.

And there was no reason why he shouldn't forget all about her. Her period had started a few hours after he and Braden had left on Saturday morning. They'd popped into her room long enough for Braden to say, "I-I'm s-orry you g-got s-ick," then they'd left. Mark had promised to call. And he probably had, but she'd been so miserable and — she had to admit—*disappointed* that she hadn't left her bed even to answer the phone.

Her sisters had practically force-fed her chicken soup and that astringent-tasting concoction of Liz's.

"It's called *kombucha*," Liz had told her when she'd

visited a few hours after Mark and Braden had left. "It's made from fermented mushrooms and—"

"Don't," Alex had said, handing back the empty glass. "I think it might have helped settle my stomach, and I can almost tolerate the taste, but I don't want to know where it comes from."

Liz had saluted and left. She'd returned daily with a fresh glass of her mouth-puckering brew. Now, she was back again.

"Good morning. The nurse of Christmas present here," she called from the doorway. "Are you alive?"

Alex was sitting up, her feet touching the floor. She'd arisen early and taken a long hot bath, but the effort had drained her, and she'd returned to bed in fresh pj's. She hadn't taken time to blow dry her hair and cringed to think how bad she looked.

"Barely," she called. The word came out as a froggy croak.

Liz stared at Alex a minute then grinned and motioned for someone to join her. "She's fine. Just about her usual feisty self."

Alex looked up. For half a second she hoped…*Mark?* But no, the man who stepped to Liz's side wasn't Mark. "Hi, David…I mean, Paul. I might be on the road to recovery, but I have days and days of cooties on my teeth so I wouldn't come any closer if I were you."

"Ewww," Liz said, scrunching up her nose. "More information than my poor fiancé needed."

"Sorry." She stared at the pair a moment. Something had happened. "You two are beaming so bright I need sunglasses. What's up?"

"We're going to India," Liz said, hopping from foot to foot in a most un-Liz-like fashion.

"Tomorrow," her fiancé added.

"But tomorrow's Christmas," Alex stated, dumbfounded.

Paul made an oh-well gesture. "Not in some parts of the world. We got a great, last-minute flight—probably because of the holiday."

Liz rushed forward, although she stopped short of hugging Alex. "We're going to meet our baby."

Alex's mouth dropped open. She scooted back on the bed to make room for her sister to sit. "How? When? Tell me everything."

Paul came closer to stand just behind Liz. Together, they talked—each filling in the other's sentences and adding so much information that Alex's head started to whirl. Apparently the child in question was *not* Prisha—the little girl Liz had wanted to adopt before the child's mother had come back into the picture. "Prisha is doing great," Liz said, "and if we have time we'll take a side trip to visit her, but we just don't know yet."

"We want to spend as much time as they'll give us getting to know our baby," Paul put in, reaching out to clasp Liz's hand.

He explained that different areas of the country have different adoption policies. "We should be able to bring her home within the year," he said.

"Her? It's a girl? That's fantastic. I'm so happy for you both." And she meant it. Her sister truly deserved this happiness. "When does your flight leave? Will you be here for the dinner at Romantique?"

For the third year, the Romani clan and many generous friends planned to provide a holiday meal for needy families. Normally, Alex would have been embroiled in the preparations these past couple of days, not hanging out in bed while others did all the work.

"We have to be at the airport by two, so we'll head over to the restaurant in the morning and do our share before we take off," Liz said.

"We both tend to travel light," Paul added with a smile, "so we'll leave our car in long-term parking and no one has to worry about picking us up when we get back on New Year's Eve."

Alex had to smile. The two were absolutely perfect for each other.

"Are you going to be well enough to pitch in?" Liz asked.

"I hope so, but I'm not sure about going to Mom's tonight. Why take the chance on giving anyone else my germs?"

Liz let out a theatrical gasp. "Alexandra Radonovic miss Christmas eve at Mom's? Impossible. You'll be there, even if we have to rent one of those clear plastic isolation tents."

"Ha-ha. But the truth is I don't feel particularly perky. You'll all have more fun without me."

Liz motioned Paul closer and whispered something in his ear. He responded by giving her a tender kiss, then he looked at Alex and said, "See you tonight, my almost-sister." A second later, he was gone.

Alex gave Liz a serious look. "You'd better watch it. Being too bossy is a good way to lose a man."

Liz kicked off her shoes and drew her legs across in front of herself. "What the heck is going on? I've never seen you this down in the dumps. Can't be your electrolytes."

The last was said with a wink that actually made Alex laugh. "Hormones," she admitted. "I started my period."

"Oh...*oh.* And you thought..."

"Not for sure. But kinda. The test said I was, but it had only been a few days since Mark and I were together, and I knew the results weren't completely accurate. Still..."

Liz reached out and touched Alex's shoulder. "Well, I do know what it feels like to think you're going to be a mother and then just like that—" She snapped her fingers. "You're not. It sucks, sweetie. And normally I'd tell you to take a week and wallow, but, sis, it's Christmas. You don't have a week."

Alex laughed. She couldn't help herself. As usual, her sister was right. "Okay, tell Mom I'll drop by, but not for dinner and not for long. Just to watch Maya open her presents."

Liz's smile seemed to say "Yeah, sure," but out loud she said, "Good. And just so you know, I left a quart of *kombucha* in your refrigerator. It'll last you until I get back from India. One glass every morning will aid your digestion and help rebuild your immune system. I promise."

But will it fix what's wrong with me and Mark? That, she feared, would take a magic potion.

MARK HUNG UP THE PHONE. All was in place for this evening. He'd talked to Grace and Liz. Even Yetta had called to personally extend an invitation to the Radonovic gathering at her house tonight. "Santa has promised to drop by, and I'm sure Braden will enjoy that," she'd said.

How could he say no? Even though he had yet to talk to Alex—he'd called and left several messages but she hadn't returned a single one—he was acting on faith that her sisters knew her better than she knew herself.

"Alex wants you there," Grace had said. "Trust me."

Trust. He wanted to believe that he and Alex had been given a second chance, but there was still so much that remained unresolved between them. Even with his life starting to get back on track, he didn't know if now was the right time to ask her to forgive him. Could she put the past behind them? Would she ever trust him again?

"I saw her a few minutes ago," Liz, whom he'd just talked to, had told him. "She's out of bed and moving around. I got her to promise she'd come to Mom's tonight. I know it would mean a lot to her if you and Braden were there."

Mark needed to hear that for himself. Getting up from his desk, he walked into the living room of his apartment where Braden was watching *Scrooged,* an old Bill Murray movie that Mark had found in Tracey's box of things. "We need to run over to the preschool for a few minutes, Bray. Can you turn that off?"

His son didn't look up.

"Braden?"

The boy made a don't-bother-me motion.

"Braden," he barked.

Mark immediately regretted his sharp tone. Braden's shoulders slumped and his head went down, as if dodging a blow that was sure to follow. Mark dropped to his knees beside his son and pulled Braden into his arms. "I'm sorry, kiddo. I didn't mean to scare you. I just wanted you to answer me."

After a few seconds, the child relaxed against his chest. "B-ut, D-Daddy, t-the b-boy talks," he said, pointing to the television.

Mark hadn't seen the movie in years. He didn't remember the story, except that it was a comedic take-off of *A Christmas Carol,* complete with ghosts of present, past and future. Since Braden seemed so intent on seeing the end of the show, Mark eased back against the sofa and watched, too.

He soon understood what Braden was talking about. A

character in the story—a young child who had been traumatized by something that had happened in his life—was
miraculously healed on Christmas eve. As Bill Murray
lifted the child in the air, the boy said Tiny Tim's mem-
orable line: "God bless us everyone."

Mark looked at his son, who was smiling with such trust
and hope on his face. His silent plea was all too obvious.
"Teach me how to say that, Daddy." Braden's speech had
been improving. His teacher and therapist were both very
encouraged, but was the little guy ready to go public?

"You know, Bray, I love you and I'm proud of you—no
matter what. You don't have to prove anything to me."

Braden's expression turned belligerent. "B-b-but…I…"

Mark waited patiently, willing himself not to fill in the
word his son was searching for. Whatever he wanted to say
wouldn't come, and the boy gave up with a sob. Mark
hugged him tight, dropping a kiss on the top of his head.
"It's okay, kiddo. We'll figure this out. I promise. Now,
what do you say we go buy some flowers for Miss Alex?"

"And c-candy?"

"Sure. That's a great idea."

Forty-five minutes later—did every citizen of Las Vegas
wait until the last day to complete their shopping?—they
finally arrived at Alex's. She answered the door after their
third knock.

"Merry Christmas," he said, presenting her with the
bouquet of red and white roses tucked between fragrant
stems of pine.

"Oh," she exclaimed. "Thank you. How sweet of you
both."

She stepped back, making room for Mark and Braden
to come in. The preschool seemed unnaturally quiet. An

upright vacuum was sitting just beyond her desk. "Don't tell me you were cleaning? You're supposed to be resting."

She made a casual gesture. "I didn't get far. Had to sit down after a few minutes. I really hate feeling weak and worn out. I'm not a good patient. Just ask my doctor."

"We won't stay long, but Braden and I wanted to check on you. Give her your gift, Bray, while I put these in a vase," he said, taking back the flowers. "Just point me in the right direction."

"Top shelf. Next to the refrigerator." To Braden, she said, "Oh, my goodness. Ethel M candy. My absolute favorite. How did you know?"

Mark smiled to himself. He could picture his son's ear-to-ear grin. Alex was good for Braden. Heck, she was good for him, too. But was he good for her?

A few minutes later, they were all three sitting in the sunny nook where the aides usually prepared the snacks for Alex's classes. Braden was kicking his feet back and forth beneath the stool. Mark could read his son's nervous energy. The boy wanted something but hadn't figured out how to ask for it.

Alex offered Braden a chocolate from the foil-wrapped box. "You know, I just saw my sister Kate arrive a few minutes ago at my mother's. Would you like me to call over there and see if Maya wants to play?"

Braden's eyes lit up and he nodded fervently.

She started to reach for the phone, but before she could make the call, the door opened and Maya raced into the house. "Auntie Alex, Auntie Alex," the little girl called. "Guess what? Santa came early. He brought Mommy a new baby."

Alex dropped the phone. "W-what?"

Mark put the receiver back on the base unit.

Maya threw herself into her aunt's arms, squirming and squealing with obvious joy. "Hi, Bray. Hi, Mr. Mark. Mommy's coming. She'll tell you, too. It's true. Santa left the new baby in Mommy's tummy to grow until he's big enough to be borned."

"He?" Mark asked.

The question gave the little girl a moment of pause, but after a second of reflection she said, "Yes. It's a boy."

Mark and Alex looked at each other but didn't have a chance to discuss Maya's obvious conviction because Kate and Rob arrived a second later. Mark stood up and held out his hand to the man he'd heard about—had even thought about calling when it had looked as if he was going to need a lawyer—but had yet to meet.

"Rob Brighten."

"Mark Gaylord. Sounds like congratulations are in order."

"Thanks. Maya's convinced Santa is to thank, but we're blaming Tahiti. Our honeymoon," he added with a telling grin to his wife.

"When did you find out?" Alex asked.

"I saw the doctor this morning. We thought about holding off telling people until after the holidays, but Maya knew something was up. She finally got it out of Rob an hour ago."

The man blushed. "I swear she should work for the CIA when she grows up. She's uncanny."

Maya put her hands on either side of Alex's face and said, "When you're well, you'll have a baby, too."

Alex blinked rapidly. The tears told him the truth. She wasn't pregnant. And Mark needed to talk to her alone. To Kate, he said, "I bet you'd like to talk to your sister, but could I have a few minutes first? Maybe Maya and Braden could hang out together while Alex and I...um, swing," he said impulsively.

"Sure," Kate said. "Rob and I came over to help tidy up the place before Alex started cleaning." She gave her sister a stern look. "Mom said you were probably vacuuming. Shoo. We'll do this."

Mark thought it was pretty great the way her family pitched in to help each other. He'd always been impressed with the closeness of the Radonovic family—impressed and unnerved. He'd worried that he wouldn't fit in or measure up.

Once they were outside, sitting side by side on the sturdy swings, he decided to be blunt. "You're not pregnant, are you?"

The chilly breeze tossed her curls. "No."

"I'm sorry."

She pushed off with her feet. "Really?"

"Really. But it's probably for the best."

Her chin dropped and her momentum slowed as her toes dug into the wet sand. "I know."

"But do you know why?" He took both rubber-coated chains in his hands and made her face him. "Because you're a teacher and a role model for a lot of impressionable young children. You set a high standard for yourself and for everyone in your life. I used to worry that I wasn't good enough, but the past few years have taught me a lot about myself."

She looked at him and waited.

"I know now that everyone makes mistakes. It's what you learn from those mistakes that matters. I learned what's important—family and love. What's not important are things you have no control over, like what other people say about you."

"Your dad?" she asked.

"Yeah. Deep down I thought he was right about me. That I'd never amount to anything. But he never really knew me, Alex. He was too drunk, too mean, too caught up in his own pain. Same as Odessa. Tracey finally managed to get out from under her mother's thumb and, in a way, her death made me see that I could make a clean break with the monsters in my life, too."

He explained about the investigation that had led them to Tracey's friend Pigeon. "Tracey didn't go to that house to buy drugs. She went there to take a stand. To help a friend. To close a chapter of her life that her mother had opened for her. Odessa finally admitted that Tom-Tom, the guy who was cooking the meth, had supplied her with drugs for years. He'd also raped Tracey when she was a young girl."

"Then Tracey didn't sleep with him when you…"

"No. Definitely not. Braden is my son. Statistically improbable given the one time we were together, but when you're a macho guy like me…" He grinned so she'd know he was teasing.

Her laugh was musical. "I'm glad, Mark. This is great news about Tracey. Now, you never have to be uncomfortable talking about her to Braden. He'll be very proud of her someday."

He nodded. "I plan to make sure of it."

She touched his cheek. "We should go back in."

"We still have a lot to talk about."

"I'm cold, and I just got over the flu. My mother is expecting me—and you, I've been told—to show up at her house tonight."

Mark knew she was right about getting her back inside.

Her cheeks were pinker than usual. He pulled her to her feet and was about to kiss her when she wrenched away crying, "Germs."

Something told him that was an excuse, but he'd let her hide behind that alibi for now. The past was more or less out of the way. They'd deal with the present as it came at them tonight. But after Santa's visit, he planned to broach the subject of their future together.

Chapter Twenty-Two

Alex made sure her outdoor decorations were plugged in before she left the house. Every house in the cul-de-sac, even the two that didn't belong to Romani family members, were brightly lit, making the neighborhood seem especially festive. As a favor to her mother, nobody had a car parked on the street. The empty area was necessary for the special treat that was awaiting the children.

She pulled her knitted scarf—a gift from one of her students—a bit snugger to keep out the chilly air, then hefted the plastic bag with her gifts over one shoulder and started toward her mother's home.

Amazing scents filled the air before she reached the driveway. Kate and Jo had been cooking all afternoon. Alex had offered to help, but they'd insisted she conserve her energy.

"Like I'm some kind of invalid," she muttered softly. She'd survived the flu and her first "real" period in several years. The cramps had been manageable, and once her life was back on track, she'd think about whether or not she wanted to pursue in vitro.

Oddly, her close encounter with pregnancy had made

her think twice about becoming a single parent. Or, maybe it was what Mark had said to her today on the swings. "You're a role model for a lot of little kids."

Many of the parents who brought their children to her school were managing alone. She didn't judge them. In fact, she felt nothing but compassion for the difficult job they had on their hands. But, if she were being honest, she had to admit that what she really wanted was what her sisters had found—a partner to share her life.

Was Mark that man?

Only fear—the fear of being made a fool of again—kept her from considering the possibility. She wanted to let down her guard—to open her heart to Mark and Braden— but did she dare?

"Ho, ho, ho," a booming voice said from the street behind her. "Merry Christmas."

She whirled about. "Santa," she exclaimed. "You scared me."

"Perhaps that's because you haven't been a good girl this year," the large-bellied man in a red suit and full, shiny white beard said. From his lack of stature—and because her mother had warned her ahead of time—Alex knew the portly character was her uncle, Claude.

She put down her sack and rushed to him, hugging him soundly. "Oh, Santa, you know better than that. I'm Saint Alex, in some circles."

Her uncle's hearty laugh touched her deeply, giving her the first real taste of holiday spirit. The merry twinkle in his eyes was probably from the many Christmas lights on the eaves of the houses, but for a second, she almost saw her father behind the lush beard and mustache. "Well, if that's true, then I expect you'll be getting a very special gift beneath your tree tonight, my dear. Very special, indeed."

She laughed and patted his shoulder. "So, you got my letter, then? You know what I want?"

His white gloves squeezed her arm and, keeping in character, he said, "That I do, my girl. That I do. Now, I must be on my way. The rein-ponies are waiting."

"Rein-ponies?" she repeated. He just waved and kept walking. His black cowboy boots clicked on the sidewalk.

Her mother had mentioned something about Claude rigging up his pony cart to resemble a sleigh. Her heart suddenly felt lighter than it had been in days; she picked up her bag and went inside.

"Hey, everybody, I just bumped into a guy in a red suit outside. Who's got the number for our Neighborhood Watch?"

Children's squeals and shouts echoed throughout the house as Maya, Luca, Gemilla and half a dozen second- and third-cousins stampeded to the windows to look for Santa.

"Way to go, Alex," Grace teased. "We were just gonna feed them."

"Sorry," Alex said, handing her bag of wrapped gifts to Gregor. In a soft voice, she asked, "How come you're not out helping with the sleigh?"

"Nick and Mark volunteered so I could stay with Mary-Ann," he answered in an equally quiet tone.

Mark's here already? She glanced around and, sure enough, there was Braden standing between Luca and Maya peering out a window. And sitting on the sofa, as demurely as a princess, was Gregor's wife. She scooted forward slightly, looking interested in what the children were doing.

"Wow. MaryAnn looks great," Alex whispered. "Better than great. She looks like her old self."

Gregor beamed as if Santa had handed him the best gift of all. "I know. I think she's going to make it. I really do."

Alex gave him a quick hug then dashed to the couch to talk to the woman she'd once considered a dear friend. They'd lost a lot of the closeness over the years—from work and pressures only MaryAnn truly understood, but Alex was determined to be a better friend to MaryAnn in the future.

"Welcome home, stranger," she said, sitting down. "Santa really has granted us our collective wish—to have you back, safe and sound."

MaryAnn smiled tearfully. "Thank you, Alex. It's good to be here. I honestly wasn't sure this day would ever happen, but Gregor promised me it would, and I guess that's what I needed—someone who really believed in me."

They talked a bit longer, until Grace walked into the room and shook one of Alex's sleigh bells to get everyone's attention. "Dinner is served," she said theatrically, then added, "Santa won't come until the last plate is in the dishwasher, so let's move it, people."

MARK HELD THE LEATHER HALTER of the pretty little pony with no small amount of trepidation. The ornery beast had tried to take a nip out of his leather jacket a few minutes earlier. "Listen, the antlers weren't my idea, okay? You don't have to take it out on me. I'm just trying to fit in here."

The animal shook its head, which made the felt-and-wire contraption tilt forty-five degrees to the right. Mark didn't try to fix it. Served the nippy little rein-pony right, he thought.

"Are we going to have to stand here all night?" he asked the volunteer wrangler across from him.

"God, I hope not," Nikolai said. "Did you smell the food in Yetta's kitchen? My stomach's growling so loud these beasts are going to think a wolf is after them."

Mark liked Nick. They'd had several phone conversations about what being a cop in Las Vegas might be like. He gathered that Nick was seriously considering Zeke's offer.

Curiosity got the better of him. "So, what did Grace say when you told her about the job?"

There was just enough light in Gregor's backyard for Mark to see the grin on Nick's face. "It wasn't so much what she *said* as what we did to celebrate. The *I Dream of Jeannie* bottle was really rockin'."

"I beg your pardon?"

He coughed delicately. "Sorry. Take a peek inside Grace's trailer sometime. The little one behind Yetta's house. You'll understand. In the meantime, let's just say we didn't spend the time house-hunting, but we will. Soon. She plans to tell her sisters tonight."

"Do your parents know?" Zeke had explained about Nick's situation back in Detroit.

"Not yet. They're flying in the day after tomorrow. We'll have plenty of time to talk, but I know they'll be fine with it. They want whatever makes me happy."

"They sound like really decent people. What about your birth father? Where's he?"

"Jurek and Rip got here this afternoon. Rip is my dog. They're staying next door at Claude's. Maya insisted on taking Jo's pooch over to meet Rip. They got along okay, but I'm a little worried about what might happen if he gets out. He's a city dog. Never seen a horse."

"That's *rein-pony*. Get it straight."

The two men shared a chuckle. A few minutes later, they were relieved of duty by Gregor's older brothers. "Better hurry," the eldest, whom Mark remembered meeting years before, said. "The kids inhaled their food, but Grace told them Santa wouldn't arrive until the dishes were done."

"She's tough," Mark said to Nick.

"You better believe it. Has a bullet wound to prove it."

Mark was a little surprised by how easily he'd been accepted by the other men. No one seemed to question his presence, even though he hadn't arrived with Alex. Yetta had asked him to come early so she could have a little quiet time with the children before the festivities started. That was how he'd wound up playing stable boy.

Now, he was cold, starved and anxious to see Alex.

And suddenly there she was, handing him a plate and a rolled-up napkin filled with cutlery. "That's a pretty red nose you've got, Rudolph," she said with a grin.

"Thanks. Donner and Blitzen send their regards." He lifted one foot to check for proof. "Literally."

Her laugh made him instantly warm and happy. "Save me a spot, and I'll find you in a minute," she said. "Braden and the other children are eating in Maya's room."

He was delighted and relieved to hear that his son was being included in the children's activities. Moving along the chow line, he helped himself to Cornish games hens, ham with crackling cranberry sauce, rosemary-garnished potatoes, vegetables that looked too pretty to eat and a dozen side dishes.

"Punch?" Grace, who was manning the refreshment table, asked. "We have virgin and not-so-virgin."

"Virgin, thanks," he said. "So when's the big announcement."

"What announcement?" Liz, who was next to him in line, asked.

Grace groaned and handed him his glass. "Way to go, Mark." But he could tell she was teasing. A moment later, she let out a loud, dramatic sigh. "I guess now."

She grabbed her future husband's arm, nearly making Nick drop his heavily loaded plate, and dragged him to the open archway between the living room and dining area. "Everybody. If I could have your attention a minute."

Alex cut through the chatter with a whistle that made the entire group stop talking.

"Thanks, Alex. Okay. I just thought you should know that my amazingly generous, fabulously thoughtful and caring fiancé gave me the best present anyone has ever given me this afternoon."

"There are children present, Grace. Keep it clean," a voice called out.

Grace stomped her foot. "Oh, for heaven's sake, Gregor, grow up. Nikolai told me that he's going to take over Zeke's job when he retires in a couple of months. We're moving home."

The place erupted in chaos. Mark couldn't quit grinning, which made eating rather problematic, but the food was so good, he managed.

Three hours later, after the mock sleigh rides with Santa *Claude* and the rein-ponies and a fairly well-orchestrated gift exchange, Mark sought out Alex. He'd been watching her all evening and could tell she was starting to fade.

"Kate, would you mind keeping an eye on Braden? I

think I should walk your sister home. And congratulations on the new addition."

"Thank you. We're really excited—even though Maya is convinced Santa—not Rob—is the father." They both laughed, and then she added, "Take your time. The kids are all immersed in their gifts. We won't be able to get out of here for hours."

Mark double-checked on his son before seeking out Alex. Indeed, Braden and Luca were shoulder-to-shoulder building some kind of futuristic war machine with plastic interlocking blocks.

Alex, he discovered, was still in the kitchen with her mother, putting away dishes. He went to Yetta first. "Thank you so much for having Braden and me tonight, Mrs. R. This could have been a tough holiday for us, but you and your family really made us feel welcome." He kissed her hand.

"Oh," she said with a flustered little laugh. "You always were such a gentleman. I'm sorry Ernst was so hard on you. I think you reminded him too much of himself."

"I take that as a compliment," Mark said. "Now, if you don't mind, I'm going to run off with your daughter—before she has a relapse."

Alex put up a halfhearted protest, but her mother seconded Mark's suggestion. "You know her well. Always doing for others and not herself. She needs someone to remind her who comes first."

Mark agreed, and he had a sense that they both knew he was that someone.

"Will we see you tomorrow at Romantique?" Yetta asked, as Mark took Alex's hand and started toward the door.

"Absolutely. Braden and I are both looking forward to

joining the serving line. I've had more than my share of good fortune recently and I can't wait to give a little back."

Alex was too tired to object very heartily when Mark helped her into her jacket. Naturally, it took another half hour to say goodbye to everyone, but he patiently followed her from room to room.

"You really don't have to walk me," she told him once they were on the street.

A fancy white horse trailer, fully loaded with ponies—sans antlers—was parked in front of Gregor's house. One or two of the spunky little beasts gave a whinny as Mark and Alex passed by.

"Claude really gets into the role of Santa, doesn't he?" Mark observed.

His hand felt good holding hers, despite the gloves they'd both donned. "Ever since Dad died, Claude has sorta risen to the occasion. The sleigh-on-wheels is a new addition, but I think the kids really had fun."

"I know Braden did. He's never been around animals much, so this was pretty exciting."

Alex had observed both father and son all evening and had been impressed by how well they fit in.

The cheerful lights provided plenty of illumination to see to unlock her door. She assumed he'd want to get right back to the party and his son, but instead he stepped past her and pulled her inside, too.

"Aren't you—?"

"Going back? Pretty soon. I'm not done giving gifts."

Alex frowned. She'd already given Mark his present—a novel she'd heard him discussing with Zeke and a DVD set of an old sitcom they'd been devoted fans of when they'd been dating. In return, Braden had helped her unwrap a fabulous pair of opal earrings. "I—I…p-picked 'em," he'd said proudly.

"But you already gave me my present." She started to reach up to touch her earlobe, but he grabbed her hand and led her down the hall to her suite of rooms. Grace had brought in a tiny pre-lit tree to cheer Alex up while she was sick. The miniature lights cast a festive—and rather romantic—glow.

"Can I get you a cup of tea?" she asked.

Mark laughed. "No. I'm still stuffed from dinner, but even if I wanted something, this isn't the time."

"It's not?"

"Alex, I probably haven't earned the right to ask you this—not yet, anyway, but being around you the past few weeks has shown me how empty my life is without you in it." He pulled something out of the pocket of his coat and said, "I love you, Alex. You're the only woman I've ever loved, and even though I don't deserve it, I'm asking for a second chance."

He opened his fingers to display a small gray velvet ring box. It looked used, and a bit worse for wear. Her intuition made her throat go dry; her heart started to beat erratically. *It couldn't be.*

"Open it."

Her hands were shaking so badly she could barely pry up the lid. There, on a bed of white satin was the engagement ring she'd first worn so proudly eight years earlier. A three-quarter-carat diamond in a simple setting of white gold. The prettiest one in their price range.

So many emotions hit her at once she had trouble finding her voice. "You didn't give this to Tracey?" she finally asked.

Mark crushed her to him. He shook his head. "I was

afraid you might have assumed that, but, no, sweetheart, never. Not in a million years would I have given your ring to another woman. It hurt so bad when you sent it back to me I almost threw it in Lake Mead, but I couldn't do that, either. I kept it in a safety deposit box that I opened at the bank in my name only."

She pushed free of his hold and turned on the overhead light. "It's been so long I've forgotten what it looks like," she said, sitting down on the end of her bed.

As she studied the simple design, a memory flicked to life. The two of them shopping at a jewelry store that claimed to offer the best prices in town. "I don't want some fabulous rock that I'm afraid to wear to work, Mark. Just something simple and honest and affordable. We'll buy each other gaudy jewels for our fiftieth anniversary."

"We could have it reset," Mark said. "Styles have probably changed. I wouldn't know. I'm not exactly—"

She stopped him. "Mark. I don't think so."

"Why? I know you still love me. I feel it."

She couldn't deny the truth. "I do. I don't think I ever stopped loving you, although Lord knows I tried."

"Is it because of the past?" He dropped to both knees in front of her. "Alex, I was a stupid, frightened kid the first time around. I've grown up—not because I wanted to but because I had to. Going through a divorce was a real eye-opener. Tracey and I saw three different marriage counselors. I didn't learn anything that could save my marriage, but I learned a few things about myself. I know I'm not perfect, but—"

"It's not you, Mark. It's me. I don't even know for sure if I can have kids. If the cysts come back, I might have to go back on the pill. And if they don't come back, the scarring might be too bad..." She looked down at the ring. "I'm not the same woman I was the first time you proposed to me."

He stood up and pulled her to her feet. "I'm bringing you one child, Alex, and you're giving me twenty or thirty more at the Dancing Hippo. If that's all the kids we ever have, then think how blessed our life will have been."

"But—"

"Alex, marry me. Please. I don't deserve you, but I do love you, and I promise I will never give you any reason to question that love."

She looked into his eyes and saw the future. Her first honest-to-goodness Romani vision. Christmases, births, christenings, weddings, graduations, funerals. All the images of life unfolded before her, and always at her side was one man. This man.

"Yes," she said, blinking away her tears. "Yes."

He let out a soft hoot of joy. "When?"

"I...I don't know. Grace has finally decided on May twelfth for her date. And I don't know what Liz plans to do. She's such a loner she might just elope, but I suppose I should ask her before we decide—"

"New Year's Day," Mark said with conviction.

"A week from tomorrow? Are you crazy?"

"Why not? Your family will all be here. Liz and Paul are only going to be gone a week, right? Nick's parents are flying in. And, most importantly, you and Braden and I can start making a life together. Why wait?"

"Do we need to talk about this with Braden?"

Mark whirled about and picked up the phone. Her mother's speed-dial number was listed at the top. A few seconds later, his son came on the line.

"Braden, I just asked Alex to marry us. She wants to

know how you feel about that. Do you have something you want to tell her?"

Alex's heart was thundering. She hated to put the little boy on the spot like that with all of her family around in the background. She took the receiver. "Braden, honey, it's okay. You don't have say anything now. Your dad and I will come back over and we can talk in private."

There was a pause, then, in a clear voice, unfettered by hesitation or doubt, she heard him say, "I love you, Alex."

Tears filled her eyes as she looked at Mark. "I...l-love you, too, Braden."

Mark took the phone from her hand and said to his son, "Good job, buddy. All that practicing paid off. I think the answer is yes."

A loud cry of rejoicing echoed over the line, followed by a seemingly endless line of family members who wanted to extend their congratulations. Mark handled each one with finesse—and made sure that everyone knew about the wedding that would take place in just seven days. Finally, he told whoever was on the line, "I'm hanging up now. I have to kiss my bride-to-be."

And he did.

Epilogue

The wedding was simple; the party afterward considerably more involved. First, there'd been the matter of a big enough venue. Kate and Jo had offered to use Romantique, but between cops, firefighters, preschool families and Romani, the list of guests quickly numbered more than the restaurant could hold. Fortunately, Grace had come up with an idea.

"Remember when I was going to use my trust fund to remodel the dining room at Charles's casino?" she'd told her family the day after Christmas. "Well, guess what? On a hunch, I contacted Charles's ex-partners, the Salvatore brothers, and, believe it or not, they went ahead with my idea. Gave the Xanadu a complete makeover. But the contractors fell behind schedule, and they couldn't open on New Year's Eve as planned. The work is all done, but the health department hasn't signed off on the permit so they can't use the kitchen. Which means we can hold a private party there. We just need to bring our own food."

Yep, Grace was definitely back in town, Alex thought as she and Mark greeted their guests at the post-nuptial reception and dance in the hip new restaurant.

They'd exchanged vows two hours earlier at the Dancing Hippo. Not the most romantic setting, perhaps, but Alex had felt a sense of coming full circle, since this was the house she and Mark had originally planned to buy together.

Soon, it would be their home—until their family grew. She still hoped to have a baby of her own, but even if that never happened, she was thrilled to be Braden's mother.

"Where's our boy?" she asked the man beside her.

"With Maya," Mark said. "Hopefully not picking any-one's pocket. We had a long talk about what is acceptable conduct and what isn't—a concept apparently lost on your uncle Claude."

Alex laughed. Poor Mark. He'd just married into a fam-ily rich with traditions—some less noble than others. But the Romani way of accepting and embracing newcomers was very much alive, she thought, as she watched Lydia and Reezira talking to their dates, two handsome young brothers whom they'd met at school.

At another table, Jo was sitting beside Rob's father and his lovely young wife, who was holding their baby girl, Daisy Josephine. Grace's future in-laws were nearby, along with Nick's sister and her family, who had flown in to sur-prise Nick. Nick's nieces were deep in conversation with Jurek, the man who had, in a way, made this convoluted connection possible.

Alex shuddered to think what might have happened if her mother hadn't contacted Jurek for advice when her Gypsy intuition had told her her family was in jeopardy.

"Alex," Grace said, rushing up to her. "You'll never guess what just happened. Walter and Ralph—the two brothers who own the casino—asked if I'd be interested in managing this restaurant for them."

Somehow Alex wasn't surprised. "What did you tell them?"

"That I might—if they'd consider changing the name of the restaurant to Too Romantique." She threw back her head and laughed. "Would that not be the weirdest twist of fate you've heard yet?"

No, Alex thought. What defied logic was the fact that she and her three sisters had all found love within twelve months of each other. Those kinds of odds would have made the bookies in Vegas dizzy, but when Alex had raised the point with her mother, Yetta had smiled her "Gypsy fortune-teller smile" and had said, "Did I forget to mention that I saw all of your prophecies in one year's time? I didn't share these with each of you until you were old enough to understand, but I knew I was going to give birth to four beautiful daughters, and I knew they would find true love."

Alex pushed the thought from her mind and responded to her sister's announcement. "Brilliant idea, Grace. What did they say?"

Grace's grin broadened. "They started fighting over who would get to tell Charles, who is still in jail as his lawyers squander the last of his personal wealth on yet another appeal."

Grace shivered, as if even mentioning her old nemesis made her uncomfortable. She glanced toward the stage where the DJ had finished setting up and pointed. "Looks like it's time for the Sisters of the Silver Dollar to do our thing. Where are Liz and Kate?" She shifted on her treacherously high heels to search for the missing members of their foursome.

"Wait," Alex protested. "Don't the bride and groom get the first dan—?"

Liz walked up to them before Alex could finish asking her question. Her flight had been delayed, and she and Paul had rushed to the casino straight from the airport and changed clothes in the suite Grace's future employers had provided for the wedding party. Both looked jet-lagged, but exhilarated. As promised, she had hundreds of digital images of their beautiful new baby girl. Carina Abigail, after Paul's mother.

"Surely you know by now not to waste your breath arguing with Grace," she said. "Let's just get this over with so Paul and I can slink off and crash."

Alex had agreed to join the Sisters of the Silver Dollar in one dance, as long as she didn't have to change into a costume. She loved her wedding dress—a simple white sheath with lace sleeves and inserts in the back and bodice. Just seeing the look on Mark's face told her she looked as beautiful as she felt.

"Okay. Fine. We'll do it, now." She kicked off her heels and handed them to her husband. *My husband.* "I promise this is the last time I have to do this…until Grace's wedding," she said, giving Mark a kiss that was filled with promise of another kind as well.

A few minutes later, a space had been cleared on the dance floor for the four Radonovic sisters. Alex wasn't worried about her performance. This time, she was dancing from the heart. She'd never felt more connected, more secure in who she was and where she fit in the world.

This was her world.

The music started, a flamenco beat of guitar and castanets. Alex looked at her sisters—Liz in a gorgeous sari, Kate in a royal-blue maternity dress that she hadn't even started to fill out, and Grace—in red, of course. Each a princess in her own way, beautiful and unique.

"Let's do this, my sisters. For Dad."

They lifted their arms gracefully and moved to a sound that had been a part of their blood, their history, since long before they were born. The audience responded with loud claps, whistles and calls of approval.

About halfway through the routine, without any outward sign of agreement, each sister twirled in step and found her husband or fiancé. The men put up a token resistance, but soon there were eight dancers on the floor. Then ten, when Maya and Braden joined them.

"Alex. Kate," Grace called, nodding toward where their mother was standing, a tall, silver-haired man at her side.

As all three sisters attempted to coax Yetta to the dance floor, Liz joined them. "Come on, Mom. This is *your* celebration as much as Alex's," she said. "You've proved that the old ways really do have meaning in our lives."

"Liz is right, Mom," Grace said. "This wedding makes you officially four for four in the prophecy business. I'm marrying my prince. Kate fixed her past so she could see the road to a brilliant future. Liz picked the man of shadows, and Braden was the key to healing Alex's broken heart. Now, we can all live happily ever after."

Alex looked at her sisters and smiled. She had a feeling nobody outside their family would believe such a story, but they all knew the truth.

"Hear, hear," Zeke said. "To Yetta." He started clapping and soon everyone joined in.

Yetta's cheeks turned a lovely, luminous shade of pink. Zeke whispered something in her ear, and she nodded, giving in to her daughters' urging to join them on the dance floor.

Alex grabbed Zeke's hand, too, and pulled him into the ever-enlarging circle.

"Daddy would have loved this," Alex said loud enough for everyone to hear. "And I think he would have approved of you, too, Zeke Martini. Welcome to the family."

Yetta's tearful "Thank you," and the tender look she shared with Zeke, told Alex other changes—and possibly even another wedding—might be coming in the future.

That was okay with Alex. Life was all about change. Her father had understood that better than anyone. Alex knew that if she peered hard enough, somewhere in this crowd of happy celebrants, she'd see him. The Gypsy King. He'd jingle his pocketful of coins in beat to the music. And then he'd look at his daughters and smile.

* * * * *

New York Times *bestselling author Linda Lael Miller is back with a new romance featuring the heartwarming McKettrick family from Silhouette Special Edition.*

SIERRA'S HOMECOMING
by Linda Lael Miller

*On sale December 2006,
wherever books are sold.*

Turn the page for a sneak preview!

Soft, smoky music poured into the room.

The next thing she knew, Sierra was in Travis's arms, close against that chest she'd admired earlier, and they were slow dancing.

Why didn't she pull away?

"Relax," he said. His breath was warm in her hair.

She giggled, more nervous than amused. What was the matter with her? She was attracted to Travis, had been from the first, and he was clearly attracted to her. They were both adults. Why not enjoy a little slow dancing in a ranch-house kitchen?

Because slow dancing led to other things. She took a step back and felt the counter flush against her lower back. Travis naturally came with her, since they were holding hands and he had one arm around her waist.

Simple physics.

Then he kissed her.

Physics again—this time, not so simple.

"Yikes," she said, when their mouths parted.

He grinned. "Nobody's ever said that after I kissed them."

She felt the heat and substance of his body pressed against hers. "It's going to happen, isn't it?" she heard herself whisper.

"Yep," Travis answered.

"But not tonight," Sierra said on a sigh.

"Probably not," Travis agreed.

"When, then?"

He chuckled, gave her a slow, nibbling kiss. "Tomorrow morning," he said. "After you drop Liam off at school."

"Isn't that…a little…soon?"

"Not soon enough," Travis answered, his voice husky. "Not nearly soon enough."

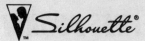

REQUEST YOUR FREE BOOKS!
2 FREE NOVELS PLUS 2
FREE GIFTS!

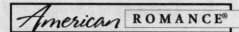

American **ROMANCE**®

Heart, Home & Happiness!

YES! Please send me 2 FREE Harlequin American Romance® novels and my 2 FREE gifts. After receiving them, if I don't wish to receive any more books, I can return the shipping statement marked "cancel." If I don't cancel, I will receive 4 brand-new novels every month and be billed just $4.24 per book in the U.S., or $4.99 per book in Canada, plus 25¢ shipping and handling per book and applicable taxes, if any*. That's a savings of close to 15% off the cover price! I understand that accepting the 2 free books and gifts places me under no obligation to buy anything. I can always return a shipment and cancel at any time. Even if I never buy another book from Harlequin, the two free books and gifts are mine to keep forever.

154 HDN EEZK   354 HDN EEZV

Name	(PLEASE PRINT)
Address	Apt. #
City	State/Prov. Zip/Postal Code

Signature (if under 18, a parent or guardian must sign)

Mail to the Harlequin Reader Service®:

IN U.S.A.	IN CANADA
P.O. Box 1867	P.O. Box 609
Buffalo, NY	Fort Erie, Ontario
14240-1867	L2A 5X3

Not valid to current Harlequin American Romance subscribers.

Want to try two free books from another line?
Call 1-800-873-8635 or visit www.morefreebooks.com.

* Terms and prices subject to change without notice. NY residents add applicable sales tax. Canadian residents will be charged applicable provincial taxes and GST. This offer is limited to one order per household. All orders subject to approval. Credit or debit balances in a customer's account(s) may be offset by any other outstanding balance owed by or to the customer. Please allow 4 to 6 weeks for delivery.

HAR06

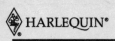

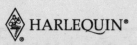

HARLEQUIN®

American **ROMANCE®**

COMING NEXT MONTH

#1141 A LARAMIE, TEXAS CHRISTMAS by Cathy Gillen Thacker
The McCabes: Next Generation
All Kevin McCabe wants for Christmas is to get closer to Noelle Kringle.
She and her son are in Laramie for the holidays, and he finds himself strongly
attracted to her. He can tell the feeling is mutual, but as quickly as Kevin's
falling in love, he can't help but wonder what it is she's trying to hide.

#1142 TEMPTED BY A TEXAN by Mindy Neff
Texas Sweethearts
Becca Sue Ellsworth's prospects for cuddling a child of her own seem grim,
until the night her old flame arrives first on the scene of a break-in to rescue her
from a prowler. Suddenly she realizes she has another chance to get Colby Flynn
to rethink his ambition to be a big-city lawyer—and to remind the long, tall
Texan of a baby-making promise seven years ago…the one she'd gotten from him!

#1143 COWBOY VET by Pamela Britton
Jessie Monroe is the last person on earth Rand Sheppard wants to rely on, but
he needs a veterinary technician—yesterday—and she's the only one for hire.
It turns out the woman who destroyed his cousin's life isn't who Rand thought
she was. And now she's all he can think about….

#1144 THE WEDDING SECRET by Michele Dunaway
American Beauties
After landing a plum position on the hottest talk show in the country,
Cecile Duletsky is ready for just about anything. Anything but gorgeous
Luke Shaw, that is. Cecile spends a fabulous night with him, knowing she isn't
ready for a complicated romance. But that's before she shows up for work and
finds Luke—her boss—sitting across from her in the boardroom.

www.eHarlequin.com

HARCNM1106